A

Tremorna

LITTLE CREEK PRESS
AND BOOK DESIGN

Mineral Point, Wisconsin USA

Little Creek Press®
A Division of Kristin Mitchell Design, Inc.
5341 Sunny Ridge Road
Mineral Point, Wisconsin 53565

Book Design and Project Coordination:
Little Creek Press

First Edition
January 2019

Printed in Wisconsin, United States of America

For more information or to order books:
email: aheyman@excel.net
or visit www.littlecreekpress.com

Library of Congress Control Number: 2018964377

ISBN-10: 1-942586-56-6
ISBN-13: 978-1-942586-56-2

Cover photo credit: © Grahammoore999, Dreamstime.com

DEDICATION
This book is dedicated to my dad, a man of quiet strength.
Miss you dad!

ACKNOWLEDGEMENTS
I want to thank author David Mudd, who was kind enough
to answer my questions about smuggling in Cornwall in the early
19th century. I also want to thank Tim Potochnik. This book
would not have been written had it not been for his
immeasurable help and encouragement.

Other Little Creek Press Books
written by Amy J. Heyman
Polvenon

CHAPTER 1

Polvenon, Cornwall – 1802

Kerena Dugan held her baby close as Jeremy scoffed, "How ye mollycoddle that boy, Kerena! He's almost two and still ye have 'im at yer breast! What's to become of 'im? Ye'll have 'im weaned within a fortnight or my name is'na Jeremy Dugan! I'm warning ye woman! Do as I say or I'll take 'im with me on the next run. Never too young to learn about 'is pa's business."

Jeremy grabbed the baby from her and held him high in the air as little Matthew howled and Kerena screamed, "Leave 'im be, Jeremy! I'll do as ye say—just leave 'im be!" Kerena tried to take Matthew, but his father held him even higher. When Kerena tearfully pleaded with Jeremy, he relented but warned her that he meant what he said.

When Jeremy left, Kerena rocked Matthew until he stopped crying and fell asleep in her arms. She was so weary. It took all of her strength to keep him fed and clothed and keep the hovel they called home neat and clean. Sleepless nights caused by worry over Jeremy's smuggling activities didn't help. What disturbed her even more was the fact that Jeremy was determined that his boy was going to smuggle as well. Kerena looked down lovingly at her baby and promised him she would never let that happen.

Later that evening, Kerena had just gotten Matthew to sleep and was looking through the front window up at the cliff path walk. She thought about how things could be if only Jeremy still worked at Polvenon Mine. She knew it was dangerous work, but at least he came home every night. When one of his best friends was injured and had to give up mining, he talked Jeremy into giving up that life too. Now they ran with a pretty rough crew making money by selling illegal contraband. There were many times when she didn't see him for a week or more. She never knew if or when he'd be home. She grew anxious when the weather was rough and prayed that the waves wouldn't capsize their pilchard boat. She breathed a sigh of relief whenever she heard his footsteps scuffling on the path, but Jeremy was a mean drunk. He would throw open the door and loudly demand a meal, no matter what time of day or night. His lewd remarks to her made shivers run up her spine. He took her roughly and grew angry when she lay there like a limp rag. His shouts would awaken Matthew, and Kerena feared her husband would hurt the baby.

This was not the life she had imagined when she married Jeremy. There was nothing she could do about it now except try to appease him in hopes of keeping Matthew and herself safe. She dreamed of taking her baby and running far away, but where would they go? How would she make a living for them?

Just then she heard Jeremy swearing outside. She knew he was angry with her and had probably gone to a pub and had too much to drink. She quickly ran into the bedroom and crawled under the quilt hoping he would leave her alone if he thought she was asleep. Luckily, he had had so much to drink that he passed out in his chair and didn't wake up until the middle of the next day.

When Jeremy awoke, he was as cantankerous as ever. He pushed Kerena away from the stove mumbling, "Ye are slow, woman ... don't know why I ever married ye ... sure ain't good for much, are ye?" Kerena felt anger building up in her but knew she needed to keep it at bay for Matthew's sake.

As Jeremy started to heat up the stew she had made the day before, Kerena asked, "Are ye goin' out again tonight, Jeremy? It would be nice if we could have an evening together—you, me, and Matthew. We never seem to—" At that moment, Jeremy turned and threw the hot ladle at her, hitting Matthew instead. Matthew screamed. Steaming juices ran down his face and neck. Kerena grabbed a towel and started to wipe, noticing the blistering already beginning to form. "Now look what you did, Jeremy! For God's sake, do what ye will to me, but leave the babe alone!"

"Oh, aye." Jeremy stated coldly and calmly. "I'll leave 'im alone, and you too, and gladly! Nothin' here for me now but the boy anyway. Don't worry yerself, woman. I won't bother ye again, but here's my promise to ye: I will be back for Matthew—mark my words well." Jeremy grabbed his overcoat, shoved some of his clothes into his satchel, and walked out the door without saying another word.

Promise or threat, his words hung in the air for hours.

CHAPTER 2

Doc Hayle checked Matthew's face and neck. "You've done wonders, Mrs. Dugan. It looks as though whatever scarring, if any, will be barely noticeable thanks to your quick thinking."

Kerena breathed a sigh of relief. "Thank you, Doctor. I only done what my ma taught me to do for burns. She was a nurse, ye know."

"Well, she knew what she was doing, and Matthew will have you and your mother to thank for that. I must be leaving now. I don't think I'll need to check in again; he's doing well."

Kerena thanked him again, and he ducked as he left through the low doorway.

Matthew fell asleep after the doctor's visit. Kerena made a cup of tea for herself and sat at the kitchen table. It had been four days since Jeremy walked out. She hadn't slept much during that time. She knew she had to leave before he returned and made good on his threat. Her first thought was to keep Matthew safe, and although it broke her heart, she knew that she needed to find a place to hide him. A plan had started to develop in her mind as she sipped her tea. She prayed it would work.

She knew she couldn't share her thoughts with anyone. Even the few friends that Jeremy allowed her to have—the wives of his closest drinking buddies—could not be told. Her isolation and despair were complete.

Kerena pulled Matthew in a wagon stolen from a nearby farmhouse. They had started out while it was still dark and managed to make it as far as Bodmin before weariness overtook her. Kerena looked around her; she'd forgotten how bleak this part of Cornwall was, with its wind-swept moors and rocky terrain. There was a heavy mist, which she hoped would hide them from prying eyes. By dusk, they reached the entrance to Bodmin Orphanage. Sobbing quietly, she lifted Matthew from the wagon, thanking God that he was asleep. She had wrapped him in some old blankets so he wouldn't catch a chill. She held him in one arm as she pulled the wagon over to a thicket, which ran behind and alongside the orphanage. Laying Matthew down, she quickly pulled brush over the wagon to conceal it. Returning to the front door, she quickly reviewed her plan in her mind: before they left home, Kerena had decided it best to give Matthew a new name. Disguising her handwriting, she had written a note to tuck into the blanket. It simply said "This is Tommy. He is my son. Please keep him safe." Kissing his forehead, she held him gently to her breast. "Don't worry, little one. The people here will take good care of you until we can be together again. Remember that your ma will love you always."

Her heart breaking, she placed Matthew on the front stoop and pounded the knocker on the huge wooden door. She looked down one more time and then ran as if the devil himself were after her.

Bodmin – 1802

Headmistress Parks of Bodmin Orphanage was notified immediately of the poor mite left on their doorstep. She told Nurse Martin to check him over and add him to the registry. A crib was secured for the new arrival. The headmistress ran to the pantry and instructed the kitchen maid to prepare some oatmeal and bring it to the nursery.

Tommy was the first baby to be left at Bodmin Orphanage anonymously. The other children were sent to them via the workhouse when the mothers couldn't care for them anymore. The young women often died from overwork or malnutrition. Their surviving children seldom fared better. These orphans needed a lot of care, as most arrived nearly starving. Tommy appeared only a bit underfed. It would be a welcome change to be able to provide for him. It wouldn't be long before they would be able to place him in a good home.

CHAPTER 3

Kerena had been walking for over four hours before she felt it was safe to stop and rest. It was midday when she reached Padstow. Dead on her feet, she sat by the side of the road eating bread and cheese she had packed when she left Polvenon. As she ate, her mind was on her next move. She had heard there was a convent nearby. It was a way for her to hide away from Jeremy and anyone who knew him. "I'll study hard and become a nun," she decided.

A rickety cart smelling of manure pulled up next to her. A bedraggled man sat on the driver's bench. "Ye comin' or goin'? I'm stoppin' in the village for a bite to eat afore I ride on up to Bude. Ye look tired and ye must be thirsty. I'm goin' to the Water's Edge Pub to down a few. Ye're welcome to come along." The smell of manure was overwhelming, but she was parched. She swallowed her disgust and thanked the man kindly as he helped her up onto the seat next to him.

The ride was bumpy and dusty, and not much was said by either until they reached the pub. Once inside, she regretted her decision. Clearly she must have looked a sight as every eye turned to stare. They found a booth near the window and ordered their drinks. She was just about to attempt small talk with this man, who said his name was John Thudd, when she overheard a conversation in the booth behind them.

"Nine years 'e got. They caught him selling 'is stolen wares down near Morna Cove."

"That's our Jeremy. 'E shoulda stuck to minin', the moron. Gives smugglers a bad name, 'e does."

Kerena heard glasses clinking and then a loud shout, "To Jeremy Dugan!" Laughter exploded followed by sniggering murmurs. Kerena couldn't believe her ears. Jeremy sentenced to nine years in prison? Could it be? Could she be that lucky?

Bude – 1802

After digesting her husband's fate, Kerena breathed a little easier. She knew she needed to continue her efforts to keep Matthew safe. Nine years in prison was a long time, but she knew her husband well. Nine years or ninety, Jeremy would come looking for her, especially as he would consider his son to be old enough to learn the smuggling trade. For now, time was on her side.

Kerena hopped onto the smelly old cart to continue with John Thudd to the village of Bude. Feeling a bit more comfortable with each other, conversation flowed between the two. She learned that although there were no "nunneries," as John called them, in Bude, there was a convent run by the Sisters of St. Peter. It was not far from Bude, in the tiny parish of Stowell.

Tired and thirsty, the two arrived in Bude. They shared one last meal together before parting ways—John on a return run to Padstow and Kerena to Stowell, which was about three hours away on foot. As she neared the village, she couldn't miss the convent. John had told her it was the tallest building in Stowell. Arriving at the old stone structure, she braced herself. She took a deep breath and rapped on the door. She hoped it would be the start of a new life for her.

CHAPTER 4

Bodmin – 1803

Tommy was almost three years old before he was adopted. He remembered little of his mother, Kerena. He seemed a normal little boy—rambunctious and curious. When he first came to the orphanage, he spoke very little. He just kept calling for his mama. A year later, he was speaking in full sentences. It seemed as though he would never stop. Headmistress Parks had been searching for a new home for Tommy for several months. It came as quite a surprise then when that knock came. Nurse Martin opened the door to a young couple. "Good morning. Is the headmistress at home?" The nurse nodded and bid them enter, offering them a seat in the narrow entrance that led to a hallway of closed doors. Headmistress Parks came out to greet them a few moments later. She led them to her office where introductions were made. "We are interested in adopting a little boy. We have no children of our own. We would like a boy who could take over our farm someday and eventually take care of us when we grow too feeble to take care of ourselves."

After spending time with Jedediah and Molly Ellis, Headmistress Parks deemed them a "perfect match" for little Tommy. The orphanage couldn't afford to be too choosy. "Donations" like theirs in exchange for children came infrequently. A week later, Mr. and Mrs. Ellis returned to the orphanage to claim him as their own.

The Ellises owned a large sheep farm on the edge of Bodmin Moor. As they rode their cart up the lane with Tommy sitting between them, Molly felt as though she was finally getting the family she'd always wanted. She loved Jedediah more than anything, but there had been something missing from her life. She was heartbroken when the doctor told her that she was unable to carry a child; she had wept bitterly. Jedediah tried his hardest to console her, but the truth was he was as disappointed as she. Looking out over the land he'd inherited from his father and his grandfather, it was important to him to have an heir to continue the farm.

"Lemme be!" Tommy squirmed, trying to break free from Jedediah's hold as his new father lowered him to the ground. He was almost four years old and didn't need any help getting out of the cart. As soon as his feet touched down he took off over the moors, luxuriating in the wide-open stretches of heath. Never before had he felt so free! Barely remembering his life in Polvenon, all he could think of now was how closed in he had felt within the walls of the orphanage. He breathed in deeply all the richness of the moors—the wild purple heather, the damp, earthy smell of peat, and fresh breezes blowing through the tall, golden grasses.

From behind him, Tommy heard Molly calling out to him to come back. Reluctantly, he turned and trudged slowly toward the Ellises and his new home.

Even at his young age, Tommy knew from the start that something was unsettling about his adoptive parents. They were overly attentive to his needs, and he felt smothered. Every chance he could, he would run down the lane or skip onto the moors and lose himself in the wonderment of nature. He loved being outdoors.

When Tommy turned four, Jedediah told him that he was now ready to take on some of the easier chores on the farm. Tommy resisted at first but soon found that he actually enjoyed the duties that kept him away from the farmhouse and out from under Molly's constant watch. She hovered over him every chance she got, hoping for some sign of affection from the boy. Tommy felt her cloying ways very uncomfortable and would often run to his room and close the door.

One morning, Jedediah took Tommy up to the moors where the sheep were grazing. He explained that the duties of a sheepherder were to ensure that all sheep were accounted for at all times and protected from attacks from wild dogs, foxes, and badgers. For several weeks, Jedediah and Tommy watched over the herd together.

The time came when the hay was ready to be cut and stacked in the barns to dry out before baling. Tommy was sent up to tend the sheep while Jedediah worked in the fields. He told Tommy he would be only a shout away.

Time passed, and Tommy grew bored. He wished he could go and explore more of the moorland. He didn't like being tied down to one spot, watching "silly old sheep." He started to wander off, admiring the skylarks diving for insects among a sea of blue bilberry. He sat on a flat rock to listen to all of the strange, new sounds emanating from the spongy bogs he was told not to go near.

It seemed like hours later when Tommy finally wandered back to the sheep herd. Jedediah was standing there looking stern. "Well, young man. I just accounted for all of the sheep—lucky for you. Where have you been? I have told you time and again how dangerous it is to wander the moors. You could have sunk in a bog, and no one would ever know what happened to you. Clearly you are too young and not ready to be left alone up here."

Tommy was repentant but insisted that he was old enough. Jedediah hid a grin and said, "We'll see. You must promise me that you will never leave the sheep alone."

Tommy hung his head and promised. "Good, now come and help me get the last of the hay in, and then we'll see what your ma has for us to eat."

Tommy was relieved that he was not going to be punished, but oh how he hated it when Jedediah referred to Molly as his ma! He didn't know what he wanted in a ma, but he knew what he didn't want.

It had been almost a year since the Ellises had adopted Tommy. He had become a little hellion. He came and went as he pleased, was late for meals, and left his chores half done. He had never taken a liking to Molly, making it clear he did not want to be touched. One day Jedediah caught him in a blatant lie. He had asked Tommy if he had milked their cow, and Tommy looked him straight in the eye and said, "Sure did." Then off he went to play on the moors. Later, Jedediah went to the cow barn and found poor Clara bawling and stomping her feet, clearly in pain and discomfort. He immediately began to milk her, hoping her udders were not already infected.

That night Jedediah sat Tommy down and confronted him with his lie. He explained how Clara's udders could become diseased, and she could die if not milked regularly. He asked Tommy why he lied, and Tommy shrugged his shoulders and said, "I don't like that stinky ol' barn, an' I don't like stinky ol' Clara!"

Jedediah and his wife finally came to the end of their rope when Tommy neglected to shut the gate of the chicken pen. They found the hens scattered all over the moors. Foxes had killed some of them. After another lecture, Tommy came right out and told the Ellises that he "don't like it 'ere." He began to cry and said, "I want to go 'ome!" The Ellises looked at each other, dismayed.

Later that night Molly told Jedediah that she wanted him to take Tommy back to the orphanage. Things were not working out like she thought they would. There was a distance between Tommy and Molly that would never be bridged. "It's better to do it now while he's still young than to have him grow up hating us." She began to sob, and Jedediah, distraught and defeated, agreed.

The next morning they told Tommy they were taking him 'ome. By the way his little face lit up, they knew they were doing the right thing. Molly said her goodbyes, tears running down her cheeks as Tommy actually gave her a quick hug. She waved as Jedediah and Tommy drove off in the cart. Tommy didn't look back.

Jedediah and Tommy arrived at the orphanage in Bodmin to find that they were not able to return Tommy. Headmistress Parks was very sorry to hear that it didn't work out for him with the Ellises. She was surprised to see that Tommy had grown so much in so short a time. Looking at him sadly, she said, "I'm afraid that we have no room for you here, Tommy. There are no beds available. We've taken in four new children since you've been here."

Tommy looked down, tears in his eyes. "Please take me back. I won't be no trouble—honest I won't." The headmistress took him in her arms as he started to sob. She looked up at Jedediah and told him of an orphanage in Tremorna that would likely take him.

Holding Tommy away from her she said, "It would be a very nice home for you, Tommy. It's much larger than our orphanage. I'm sure you'd make a lot of new friends there. Do you think you might like that?"

Tommy sniffled and nodded. He leaned over to whisper to the headmistress, "Anythin's better than a stinky ol' farm!"

Stifling the urge to laugh out loud, Headmistress Parks told them she would be right back. A few minutes later she handed Jedediah directions to Tremorna Orphanage. She also gave him a short letter she wrote to inform the Reverend Mother there of Tommy's circumstances. Shaking Jedediah's hand, she leaned down to give Tommy one last hug and wished him well.

Nearly two days later they reached Tremorna. Sister Agnessa answered the door herself. After introducing Tommy and himself, Jedediah handed her the letter from Headmistress Parks. After skimming the letter, the Reverend Mother welcomed Tommy to his new home. She told him, "We certainly do have room for a wonderful little boy like you, Tommy. Headmistress Parks says that you were well behaved during your stay in Bodmin."

She thanked Mr. Ellis for bringing Tommy to them and told him not to worry. He would be well taken care of until they could find a home more suitable to his needs. Tommy looked up at Jedediah and, once again in his short life, said goodbye.

CHAPTER 5

Stowell – 1808

Kerena had been studying with the Sisters of St. Peter for over six years and had just taken her final vows. She decided to take the name of Sister Therese after reading about her life in the Book of Saints. Although her son Matthew was never far from her thoughts, her life had changed drastically during her time there. She was no longer the fearful servant who had shrunk under the will of her husband. She knew now that her Lord was with her always. This gave her a strength she had never experienced before. When the Reverend Mother spoke with her about her future plans, she offered Sister Therese a home with the Sisters of St. Peter. During her conversations with some of the other novices, Sister Therese was told of a convent that was not a convent per se, but an orphanage in the village of Tremorna run by the Sisters of Hope. Sister Therese told the Reverend Mother of her desire to go there. The Reverend Mother had watched her working with the poor children in the district and knew she had chosen her path well. So it was with the blessing of the Sisters of St. Peter that Sister Therese left Stowell. She was ready to embark on a new adventure. She still nursed the hope that someday she would hear news of Matthew. It was what she prayed for every day.

Tremorna – 1808

Sister Therese was accepted as a working nun at Tremorna Orphanage. During her initial meeting with Sister Agnessa, the Reverend Mother of the orphanage, it was decided that she would be assigned the duties of a recordkeeper. These included documenting the dates of arrival and departure of each child and ensuring that new arrivals received personal items (clothing, shoes, etc.). Sister Therese would also be keeping financial records of donations to the orphanage, whether they were general or child-specific, and recording any pertinent information regarding adoptive parents. Although she felt her strengths would be better utilized in the care of the children, she accepted the position graciously.

Sister Agnessa had warned her that the records had not been kept up-to-date during the past year, as the former recordkeeper had left quite abruptly to take care of her sickly aunt. One morning, Sister Therese was reviewing the files on each child. She noticed that the files were not in any order, so she began to alphabetize them. It was difficult, as many of the orphans did not have a last name. She decided to put them in order according to their first names.

Suddenly Sister Therese shot up out of her chair! The file she was holding fell through her fingers, papers scattering to the floor. "It can't be!" She fell to the floor, scrabbling for the documents, trying to organize them with shaking hands. She sat down on the floor, dumbfounded. She stared at the wall for several minutes, rocking back and forth, murmuring, "My God, my God, my God ..." Attempting to pull herself together, she took a deep breath and looked down. There it was written across the top of the first page, "Thomas (Tommy) Ellis. Approximate age: four." She closed her eyes for a minute, blinking back tears, thinking of that horrible day when she left her son Matthew at the door of the Bodmin orphanage. In her past life as Kerena Dugan, she had changed his name to Tommy to make it harder for his father Jeremy to find him. Over the past six years, she had never regretted what she'd done. Yes, there may have been occasional moments of doubt, but she banished them to the far corners of her mind. Not a day went by that she hadn't thought about her son, praying for his safety. She had always hoped he would have been placed in a good home with parents who loved him.

As Sister Therese looked down at the papers, she realized he must have been adopted at one time. But what happened? How did he end up here? She rifled through the file and found that the Ellises had adopted him in 1803. He was brought to Tremorna Orphanage a year later by his adoptive father, Jedediah Ellis. Reason: "Child unsuitable" was all it said. Tears started to fall as she tried to imagine what it had been like for her son. Poor Matthew! Shuffled around so often in such a short time. "Oh God!" she moaned. "What have I done?"

That night Sister Therese lay in her bed and wept bitter tears of remorse. She longed for the lost years of Matthew's life—years she'd never get back. Her hatred of Jeremy Dugan, dulled by time, reignited. She did not allow herself the luxury of questioning her feelings for this man, even though she knew God would not approve.

CHAPTER 6

Tremorna – 1810

Sister Agnessa had possession of little Tommy's ear as she dragged him into the scullery. She sat him down none too gently in front of a mounting pile of dirty dishes. "These had better be spotless before dinnertime or you will be going without!" Tommy snorted, which only made things worse as Sister Agnessa glared and exclaimed, "That's enough sass, young man. Not a morsel will pass your lips 'til the morrow!" As Sister stomped out of the room, Tommy snorted again and threw a towel at her backside.

Tommy had lived at Tremorna Orphanage since he was four years old. At ten years of age, he was a skinny redhead with long legs that saved him from many a scrap with the law. He wore his reputation as a troublemaker like a badge of honor and was proud of his many escapes from the eyes of the preventive men—the officials who scoured the coast of Cornwall on the lookout for illegal smuggling activities. Tommy was a runner for the smugglers who used the caves below Tremorna Orphanage to stow their stolen goods.

Tremorna Orphanage was located near Holly Bay and its estuary. Built in 1788 as a prison, it was grey, dreary, and dismally cold. Bars crossed the windows of each bedroom, which were formerly cell blocks. A bleak wilderness surrounded the compound. Several prisoners had at one time started to dig a tunnel to the caves near the coast to escape. Their success resulted in the prison's demise, and those who had not escaped were transferred to Bodmin Jail. Smugglers took advantage of the time the prison stood empty, using the abandoned prison for storage. To their dismay, in 1803 it was reopened as a home for orphans. The smugglers had tried several times to sabotage the opening of the orphanage, finally relenting when nuns and homeless children occupied it.

The Sisters of Hope ran the orphanage with Sister Agnessa at the helm. Most of the children entering the orphanage were frail, half-starved, and ragged. Sister Agnessa was very strict with them, but fair and caring. She treated the staff much the same.

"Tommy, what did she catch you at this time?" questioned Winnie as she entered the scullery.

"Ah, nothin' but love 'tween Aggie and me!" Tommy laughed. "She spied me comin' in early this mornin'. Don't take to early risers, I guess."

"Now, Tommy, please don't tell me ye were out all night again. She'll have yer 'ide for sure if ye're ever caught. Take care, now. She's watchin' ye. I'll sneak some cheese and a few biscuits up to ye later. Now get to those dishes afore she comes in and finds you haven't even started."

Tommy smiled as Winnie left to help Cook prepare supper. "Winnie's a good egg, she is," he thought as he grabbed the first plate and began to scrub. Eleven-year-old Winnie Pencott often assisted Cook in the kitchen and attempted to keep the younger ones in line. Tommy knew she had a special place in her heart for him, and he loved her dearly.

Winnie looked out the kitchen window as she chopped the carrots for the soup. She smiled when she spotted Roger Hawker up on the cliff walk astride his horse. Roger was one of the riding officers assigned to this section of coast. He was a tall, gruff man but a staunch patron of the orphanage. He loved the children and often visited them when his time was his own. Often, Winnie would spy him playing with the younger ones and daydream about someday becoming his wife and having children of their own. Roger, of course, had no clue as to her feelings for him. Winnie knew she was too young to be having thoughts about this much older man, but she couldn't help herself. Liza Barnes would often tease Winnie, making kissing noises whenever she spied Winnie searching the coast. Liza was two years younger than Winnie, but they had become fast friends when Winnie had protected her during a tussle with Pudgie Jewell. He had called her "gypsy scum" and started pulling her hair. Liza was a beautiful little girl with long, dark hair and olive skin. The youngest of twelve Barnes children, she was the only one with dark skin. The other siblings took after their parents; they were fair-skinned and light-haired. Mr. Barnes would not accept that Liza was his own, claiming that she was a result of a night of passion between Mrs. Barnes and a traveling gypsy.

"Ye'll cut yer fingers off if ye don't watch what ye're doin', missy!" declared Tessa, the head cook.

Winnie sighed long and loud, turning back to her chore. "Yes, Cook," she replied as she smiled at Tommy, who was still staring at a huge stack of plates.

"When I grow up, I ain't gonna have no dishes in my 'ouse!" Tommy exclaimed. "Just a pot and a fork— mebbe a spoon!"

"And 'ere I was savin' up to buy a silver tea set an' perty little China cups to give ye for when I come a-visitin'!" Cook released a sound that would bring the ships in from sea on a foggy night, which set all in the kitchen to giggling and screeching.

That evening, Jock Hastings crouched in his pilchard boat along the Holly Bay estuary waiting for the signal. It was a bitterly cold night with a wind that cut through to his bones. As soon as he spied a lantern lit in the upper north window of the orphanage, he gestured to his crew to row closer to shore. Their vessel was soon surrounded by men, women, and boys hurriedly but silently unloading the cargo. They carried, sloshed, and dragged the goods into the mouth of the cave that tunneled into the bowels of Tremorna Orphanage.

Much later, Jock sat in the Owler. His feet were up on the roughly hewn table, his pipe was lit, and he was listening to Whistler and Lundy relating the night's events. Jock's wife, Sal, as lank as Jock was round, ran to and fro waiting on customers late into the night. She hoped for a chance to get off her feet but found it impossible. Rubbing her lower back as she neared her husband's table, Jock snatched her up and settled her on his lap. "Git off yer feet, wife! Let the scrubwoman wait the tables awhile. Ye look dead on yer feet, luv," he exclaimed as he gave her a peck on the cheek.

Sal inherited the Owler from her father, and she ran it as a warm, cozy inn. It had two bedrooms upstairs, which were let to travelers. Another, behind the kitchen on the main floor, was where Jock and Sal resided. An enormous fireplace warmed the dining room. Surrounding it were benches along the walls and tables and chairs in the middle. Along the inside wall, just in front of the kitchen entrance, ran a long bar. It had been built from the wood of an old lugger, stools spanning the length.

"Eh, that Tommy'sss a grand lad! Sssneaky and connivin', he'll be one of uss afore you know it," cackled Harry Drake, a well-known local free-trader. He teamed up with Jock and Lundy and the rest of Jock's crew to transport contraband to secret coves and bays all along the southwest Cornish coastline. Losing his front teeth in a raid years before had earned him the nickname Whistler. His s's were pronounced and sharp.

Lundy Mann downed his grog in one long, noisy swig. "Long as Tommy don't get caught, we'll be a'right," he said. "Next time 'e mayn't be so lucky." Jock and Whistler, however, were lucky to have Lundy as a friend. He knew the Channel Islands like the back of his hand. He had a quick wit and was always ready with a bawdy line.

"Well boys," sighed Jock, as he gently pushed his half-sleeping wife off his lap. "It's off to bed with me, and so time to close the Owler for the night. May the good Lord keep ye 'til the morn," he said as he lifted his glass one more time in a toast to the evening's success.

CHAPTER 7

The children's quarters were located on the second floor of the orphanage. The bars of each cell block had been removed, and walls with doorways replaced them. The rooms were small, so each child had their own. There were accommodations for sixty children, but the building currently housed thirty-five. Sarah and Liza's rooms were next to each other, and Winnie's room was just down the hall. Down another corridor, Billy and Pudgie were next door to each other, and Tommy was a few rooms down. With rooms next to each other, it was easy for the children to have conversations when not together. The children often played in the empty cell blocks. A larger room at the end of the corridor, which was most likely an old guardroom, was the classroom where Sister Matias attempted to teach ABC's and figures.

That evening as promised, Winnie delivered a small supper to Tommy, and he gobbled it down. "Aw, thanks, Win! Sure starvin' I was. Ye're always good to me, Win. I don't deserve it."

"That's right, ye don't!" Winnie said as she laughed and lovingly hit him upside his head. "Sister Agnessa is in the kitchen right now inspectin' yer handiwork."

"I scrubbed 'em good enough for the king to eat off. Old Aggie won't find anythin' to whip me for," Tommy laughed as he licked his fingers and handed the plate back to Winnie, thanking her again.

"Can ye keep it down o'er there? Some of us are tryin' to catch some winks afore the morn," Pudgie complained.

"Sorry, Pudge," Winnie whispered as she tiptoed past his room.

As Sister Matias stood in front of her class the next morning, Pudgie looked longingly at her. She was very beautiful. He softly sighed. As much as Pudgie enjoyed taunting Billy and making the girls squeal with his antics, he treated Sister Matias with the greatest awe and respect. "No one that lovely should be a nun," Pudgie often thought. He never liked authority figures and had his run-ins with them fairly often. He always made sure though that he stayed on the good side of Sister Matias. His mother died giving birth to Pudgie, and his father couldn't take care of him. At age ten, he towered over most children his age, and his stick-like figure had earned him the nickname Pudgie.

"Now class, let us open our grammar books and start where we left off yesterday. Tommy, sit up straight. Liza, stop squirming and please pull your hair back away from your face so you can see what you're reading." Sister sighed audibly and started the lesson. Sometimes she wondered if she was ever getting through to these dear orphans. Billy, a heavyset little boy with curly, brown hair, was smart as a whip, but he had a very pronounced lisp. Because of this, the other children assumed that he was dull-witted. They teased him about it mercilessly. Tommy often mimicked him cruelly, which caused Billy to withdraw even more. He would sit at his desk with his head down and pray that Sister Matias wouldn't call on him. She was very sensitive to Billy's speech problem and seldom asked him to participate. However, it was hard not to when no one else in the class volunteered.

Winnie often assisted Sister Matias in keeping the younger children in line. She helped Sarah with her figuring, turning each problem into a little story, so it was easy for her to understand. Sarah was a happy-go-lucky four-year-old whose parents gave her up when she was born. They had no money to care for her, and so she never knew any other home. Sarah was often ignored, being the youngest, but she allied herself with Billy. She often defended him against the taunts of Pudgie and Tommy. As embarrassing as this was to Billy, he did cherish the friendship that had developed between them.

"Liza, would you please read the sums you've written on your slate?" Sister Matias asked. Liza stood, and as she struggled through the lesson, Tommy threw the remains of his apple at the back of Billy's head. Billy ignored it, but Liza saw it out of the corner of her eye. She fell into a fit of giggles, which didn't stop even after Sister told her to sit down and see her after class. Knowing that she no longer had the attention of the children, Sister Matias sighed heavily and dismissed the class for the day.

Father Cotter, the newly ordained pastor of the parish of Tremorna, fancied himself above the common villagers. He came once a week to try to instill some religion into the lives of the orphans. If not for his garb, he would have been very unimpressive. No one would have taken particular notice of him in passing. It was truly the clothes that made the man. In his religious costume, he assumed the mantle of dignity, authority, and goodness—perhaps even godliness.

Sister Agnessa attended Father Cotter's religion lessons along with the children. It was the only time during the week when the children were well-behaved—well, almost. She firmly believed that rescuing a child from poverty or abuse was an important step in saving their soul from eternal damnation.

As Father Cotter read from the book of Job, the children wiggled in their seats. They were uncomfortable with all of the horrid things that had befallen Job, all because God had let Satan have his way with the poor man. "Why'd God let that 'appen, Reverend? Couldn't 'e have thtopped it?" Billy quietly lisped, a tear wetting his eye. Pudgie poked Liza and raised his eyebrows. Liza stuck her tongue out at him. She felt a little sorry for Billy at that moment.

"Well, Billy," the priest responded, "yes, He could have stopped Satan at any time, but He had a plan. Through Job and his sufferings, we see that if you stay true to the Lord and trust Him through the hard times, you will receive a reward. As we read further, you will see that is exactly what happened to Job."

"Yeah, but in the meantime, 'is whole family died! How do ye ever get 'em back, huh?" Tommy spat out.

Sister Agnessa shushed Tommy as the pastor explained. "We don't know all the answers and are not meant to in this world. In the next, if we are good Christians and stay true to God, He will open our eyes so that we may understand at last."

Father Cotter ended the lesson by having the class stand and, heads bowed, recite the Lord's Prayer. While they were mumbling the words, he decided that he'd better add a Glory Be and a Hail Mary for good measure. "Can't be too careful where the Lord is concerned," he mused. The children shuffled to the dining room for their midday meal, Pudgie and Tommy pushing Billy and mocking him by pretending to cry.

CHAPTER 8

The following week, Jock's crew were set to land in the Holly Bay estuary. Even with their pilchard boat painted black and its dark sails, a sliver of moon was not their friend. Tommy's "all clear" from the orphanage window heralded a safe landing. It spurred them on toward shore regardless of any unseen danger.

"Tommy's never steered us wrong yet. Must 'ave gone searchin' an' found nothin' to stop us." Lundy whispered.

"Aye, Lundy. Reckon ye're right." Jock stood and gave the signal for the tubmen to wade out to guide the boat up on the beach. Batmen stood by to protect the cargo as it was thrown overboard onto the shingle. As Harry Drake watched, men, women, and boys surged forth out of the darkness of the cove to transport the stolen goods into the tunnel that led to the orphanage.

Just then a whistle blew, and men on horseback, lanterns suddenly ablaze, began their descent to the shore. Jock and his men knew they had only minutes to hide the contraband, climb aboard their vessel, and shove off as far into the water as possible without being seen by the preventive men. On the beach, men, women, and children scattered like roaches. By the time the riding officer and his men reached the bay, all was dark, and not a soul was in sight. The townsfolk knew the penalty for receiving smuggled goods was harsh. Cursing under his breath, Roger Hawker threw his spyglass, which landed on a jutting rock edge and shattered to pieces. This brought another curse from him. Unable to see Jock's boat, Roger and his men turned toward the beach searching for any sign of illegal activities. Jock and his men were expert smugglers and knew what they were doing. Roger already knew he would find nothing.

The next morning brought a standard breakfast: porridge with diluted milk and a glass of apple cider. Tommy twirled his spoon in the gruel, not paying attention to the chatter around him. His heart was still pounding out of his chest. Last night he'd made an error that could have cost Jock and his men their lives. "How did I not see Roger 'awker? Or at least smell 'im?" Tommy pondered. The riding officer always wore a subtly scented ointment, but Tommy could smell it a mile away. "T'weren't no wind. Why did I miss that?"

At that moment Pudgie poked Tommy in the ribs. "Whatcha thinkin' on so 'ard? Ye 'aven't 'ardly touched yer food. If ye don't want it, say so. I'm near starved, I am!" Tommy pushed his dish toward Pudgie's sticky fingers and watched as he devoured it. Ignoring Pudgie's question, Tommy left the table and went to the infirmary and was almost knocked over by the awful smell of carbolic soap. He knew he could get a few winks before Sister Hildegard came to check on her patients. Hopefully he'd wake in time to slip out unnoticed. He fell into the first vacant cot and instantly fell asleep.

Sister Agnessa had been watching Tommy during breakfast. He looked rather pale and seemed very distracted. "That can only spell trouble," the sister mumbled to herself as she followed him to the infirmary. He was fast sleep, or pretending to be, by the time she got there. At that moment, Sister Hildegard walked into the room. She looked at Sister Agnessa, who had put her finger to her lips to shush her. "Let him sleep awhile," Sister Agnessa whispered. "When he wakes up, send him to my office." With that, Sister Agnessa tiptoed from the infirmary leaving Sister Hildegard wide-eyed and feeling a bit sorry for the boy. Shaking her head, she went about her duties quietly so as not to wake him.

The sun was shining through the high windows as girls completed their chores of dusting and polishing. Some of the boys were assigned to scrub the floors, while others polished the boots of the children and staff. The lucky boys were outside enjoying the fresh air while picking fruit and weeding the huge gardens. Billy was on his hands and knees weeding between the rows of green beans, carefully checking each row to ensure he had not missed any. The last time he was assigned this task, he missed an entire row and got six heavy blows across his bare backside. He couldn't sit for several days! Punishments were rife in the orphanage, but the worst by far was being denied the festivities for that month. Anyone could handle a little pain now and then, but not going on their monthly outing was unthinkable. Billy knew that this month's day trip was on a steamer. That was something he was not going to miss!

Sister Matias came out to inspect the gardens. She loved walking among the vegetables and flowers. She had been known to get her hands dirty and assist with the hoeing or in digging holes for the many seedlings that needed to be planted. When she saw Billy, she encouraged him by shouting out to him, "Good job, Billy!" His head popped up out of the rows of beans, a wide grin across his round face. "Keep up the good work and maybe I'll read your favorite story this afternoon," Sister

Matias smiled as she continued her stroll through the rosebushes. As she neared the cove, she heard hushed voices coming from the beach below. Not wanting to eavesdrop, she moved to return to the orphanage when she distinctly heard Mary Wendron's voice. She was scolding someone harshly, telling them to be more careful in the future. "Aw, our Mary, leave off, will ya? I said I would an' I will."

Sister Matias knew that voice. It was Tommy. "Now what has he gotten into this time?" Sister wondered as she trudged back toward the gardens.

Tommy had already had his "talk" with Sister Agnessa. As usual, his answers to her questions revealed nothing, and as usual, Sister Agnessa dismissed him. She told herself she needed to keep a closer watch on him.

"Ye're not to go out tonight!" Sal lashed out at Jock. "I know I did'na marry a fool. Let things settle afore ye take up again."

"Oh aye, I'll wait a night or two, if only to stop yer yammerin', woman." Jock laughed playfully. He loved that his wife looked out for him. She didn't have a mean bone in her body, but oh how she loved to scold. He took it in stride, smiling all the while, which unnerved Sal to no end. She knew how dangerous his trade could be. Many times she hid contraband from the revenue officers in their bedroom—not in the cellars which is the first place they'd look. A hidden space behind the door in her wardrobe had worked well. So far. "Well then," Sal sighed. "At least we'll have a bit of peace for the next night or two."

Not wanting to worry Sal, Jock kept his plans to unload last night's cargo at the port near Pentruth. He would do it tomorrow night.

CHAPTER 9

Mary Wendron walked back from the cove to the cottage she shared with her mother and younger brother. She thought about Tommy and prayed that he would heed her warning. Mary was the head housekeeper at the orphanage. She was usually rather quiet and shy. This day, however, she was so worried about Tommy and his connection to Jock and his friends that she felt she must talk to him and remind him of the danger he was in. Earlier in the day, Mary had overheard a conversation between Roger Hawker and Sister Agnessa. Evidently, Roger felt that someone at the orphanage was working hand in hand with the smugglers, giving them signals in the dead of night. Sister Agnessa assured him she would get to the bottom of it. Mary knew that Sister Agnessa was already suspicious of Tommy. The nun had had reports of his late night escapades. These had come from Sister Therese, the recent transfer from the convent in Stowell. She had asked to see Sister Agnessa shortly after her arrival and had told her that she had seen a young boy leaving the building late at night. From her description, it could only be Tommy.

—◦O◦—

Later that evening, while Billy was patiently teaching Sarah how to play checkers, Liza plopped down on the rug to watch. She let her mind drift, closing her eyes in an effort to remember her brothers and sisters. She had no trouble recalling her mother. She was buxom and pink-cheeked with the prettiest blue eyes Liza had ever seen—the only physical trait Liza inherited from her. She barely remembered her father. He seemed to make himself scarce when Liza was around, often ignoring her when their paths did cross. Liza had wondered why he seemed to dislike her so, until she walked in on a terrible fight between her parents. She heard her father say that she was "no child of 'is," and wanted "no part of 'er." A week later, Liza was sent to the orphanage with the explanation that there were "just too many mouths to feed." As she was the youngest, it would be easier for her to settle in elsewhere, they claimed. Liza never regretted leaving. As much as she loved her siblings, they too treated her as if she were different. She was. She knew it. When the sisters of the orphanage welcomed her with open arms, she felt that she had finally found a place where she could be herself and not be shunned.

All these thoughts were going through Liza's head when, from behind, Pudgie grabbed her by the hair trying to lift her. Liza pulled her hair away from him, swung around and gave him a walloping kick in the shin. Startled, Sarah jumped up and upset the checkerboard, much to Billy's dismay. "Now look what you did Pudthie!" Billy cried.

"Oh grow up, ya big baby," Pudgie barked as he limped off, rubbing his leg.

Jock's plans to stash last night's take near Pentruth went without a hitch. He was back at the Owler at a decent hour listening to the crude talk of his mates and drawing pints behind the bar. Sal didn't suspect his broken promise not to go out that night. The atmosphere in the pub was lighthearted. There were many toasts to future successes. Tales of John Carter, a well-known smuggler who'd escaped arrest on many occasions, were bandied about. Lundy told of seeing a black dog a fortnight ago, which is always a harbinger of doom for the person who sees it. He laughed it off as a fanciful tale in front of his friends, but Harry had noticed a look of fear in Lundy's eyes the night before when they were almost caught with their tobacco and brandy.

"An' who'll trade their grinnin' toothless skull
for a pint o' grog, an' a sailin' man's yarn?"

The men were just starting to sing an old smuggler favorite when Tommy burst through the door. "A ship's just rammed the rocks!" he screeched. While the boy tried to catch his breath, Jock was on his feet, signaling to Lundy and Harry. He knew that the sooner they got to the beach, the more loot they could grab. Tommy knew he'd done right letting the smugglers know about the wreck first. Now he ran from house to house, pounding on doors shouting, "Shipwreck!" Townspeople heedlessly ran down the dangerous, rocky footpaths to the water's edge. Many of them jumped in to grab at floating kegs and trunks. Men brought cudgels laced with iron bands, ruthlessly swinging at the survivors' screaming, bobbing heads. They wanted no witnesses to the night's cruel raid.

Suddenly, men and women alike froze in place as the bow of the ship was wrenched and twisted off the rocks by the high waves and strong winds, making a sound akin to a banshee's mournful keening. For that moment, superstitions ran high, as the banshee only came out when death was expected. The lure of precious cargo, however, proved stronger, and so the merciless looting and mayhem continued. Women and girls who were passengers on the ship were weighed down by their long, heavy, billowy dresses. Exhaustion from thrashing about to stay afloat made them easy prey. While they were struggling to swim to shore, men held their heads underwater until they succumbed and deeply inhaled the seawater.

Tommy stood dumbstruck at the edge of the water, staring at the destruction and listening to the screams of women and children. In the moonlight, pools of blood glistened in the dark water like jet-black oil. A young boy's headless body bobbed up against Tommy's feet. Jumping back, he fell into the arms of Roger Hawker. Too stunned to fight, he let the revenue officer drag him away from the shore and dump him in a heap on the sand. Roger put one of his men in charge of Tommy as he returned to the melee, using his own weapon to batter the heads of a few looters.

Harry and Jock were tugging a heavy trunk out of the water when Jock noticed Roger walking toward Lundy, club raised. Two short, sharp whistles signaled Lundy to duck fast. He got away but ran right into the arms of Roger's men. Harry groaned as they led Lundy away. "Keep yer head, Harry," Jock said. "Lundy won't talk."

"Aye, sir—but the boy!" Harry croaked.

"Let's get this trunk stashed and worry about Tommy later!" Jock shouted over the screams and whistles.

CHAPTER 10

The next morning there were constant whispers during Father Cotter's Good Samaritan lesson. No reprimands were brought forth from either the reverend or Sister Agnessa, which was highly unusual. Although Father Cotter attempted to expound on the virtues of the Bible excerpt, his mind was elsewhere as he nervously fidgeted with a piece of chalk. Late last evening brought a loud rap on the rectory door. He opened it to Jock's pallid face and Harry's tear-stained cheeks as they barged in with a heavy, wet trunk. "Ye'll need to hide this in yer wine cellar, Father. Could'na chance our regular spot. Too many revenue men near the tunnel and did'na want to take that risk." Jock explained quickly.

Between the three of them, they managed to lug the oversized box down the cellar steps of the rectory. After stashing it behind legal kegs and bottles of wine, Jock wiped the sweat from his neck and told the priest they would be back when it was safe to transfer it. They counted on the discretion of Father Cotter as he had supported them during previous close calls. He tended to turn a blind eye to their activities in anticipation of a few bottles of their choicest brandy.

Sister Agnessa coughed discreetly to get the attention of the priest. He nodded and continued reading about the good Samaritan from the Gospel of Luke. Pudgie raised his hand and asked, "How come some of the people ignored the guy an' walked on the other side of the road? Did 'e stink or somethin'?"

At this, Sister Agnessa even stifled a giggle, but Father Cotter glared at Pudgie and answered testily, "He may have, Pudgie Jewell, but he most likely smelled better than you do today." Most days this would have triggered a room full of laughter and finger pointing. Today, Liza and Billy had their heads together, still whispering. The other children stared at their unusual behavior and remained silent too.

"Billy and Liza, would you please share whatever it is that is keeping you from paying attention to Father Cotter?" Sister Agnessa asked as she wandered toward their desks.

"Sorry, Sister." Liza began. "It's just that we noticed that Tommy is no' in class today an' 'e weren't at breakfast neither."

It was at this point that Sister Agnessa remembered what Sister Therese had told her about a little boy sneaking out the other night.

Winnie was helping Cook with the breakfast dishes when there was a knock on the back door. Winnie opened it to Roger Hawker, who looked as though he hadn't slept the night. "Good morning, ladies. I have some rather bad news. Sister Therese told me that Sister Agnessa is busy with the religion class right now, so I thought I'd come to you instead. Would you please let her know that we have Tommy and will be holding him for questioning? He may have been involved in the raid on the shipwreck last night. He was present and may know something, even if he didn't take part. I just thought someone here should know. Depending on his answers, he may or may not be coming back to you this day." With that, he tipped his hat and turned to leave.

"Is he okay, Mr. 'awker?" Tessa asked, twisting her hands in her apron.

"Aye, as far as I can see he seems fine. Good day, ladies."

Winnie burst out crying as soon as the door closed.

The weather was turning cooler as autumn approached. As leaves fell, so did the mood of the townspeople. Many felt cheated out of their portion of the goods that could have been safely stowed away if not for the raid by the revenue men. They had counted on their share to supplement meager earnings. Winter would bring hardship, as fishing and farming would drop off drastically until spring. Salting of fish and canning of fruits and vegetables began in earnest in hopes of full cellars to tide them over.

Mary Wendron and her mother had a small garden with plum trees protecting it from the salty winds. While Mary picked the last of the plums for the season, her mother was busy in the kitchen canning beans and tomatoes. Mary stopped a moment to admire the view from where she stood. She loved the gnarled trees bent by the constant winds blowing over the moors. Purple heather and pink sea thrift spread as far as the rocky headlands. Today the clouds sped by with strips of sunlight shining through, dancing on the water.

"Breathtaking, isn't it?"

Mary spun around to see the smiling face of Roger Hawker. He stood tall, the wind blowing through his ebony hair. Mary's heart raced. She had fallen in love with Roger the moment she first saw him. It was two years ago when he began to visit the children at the orphanage. He joined right in with whatever games they were playing, acting like a child himself and enjoying it immensely. The children loved him. That day Mary had found him crawling around on the ground giving piggyback rides and later teaching them funny little magic tricks. Roger was known throughout the area as a strict, rather gruff preventive officer who took his duties very seriously. It was refreshing to Mary to see another side of him.

She hadn't expected Roger to stroll into her garden as he did. He had never even visited her at her home before. Mary finally found her tongue. "Yes. It truly is."

"I'm sorry if I'm intruding. I just stopped in at the orphanage to give Sister Agnessa some bad news. Tommy was taken into custody last night as he may have been involved in the horrible plunder and murder on the beach."

"No!" Mary gasped. "Is he okay?"

"A little shaken, but on the whole doing well. I'm not sure that he actually took part, but he was found standing near the water. We are hoping that he can at least enlighten us about what happened. He may know who was involved, although knowing Tommy, he wouldn't betray a trust."

Mary nodded. "Yes, you are right. He won't tell—unless they hurt him to get answers?"

"No. None of my men would be instructed to harm a child," Roger explained. "I'm sure he will be sent back to the sisters within a day or two."

"Thank you for letting me know, Mr. Hawker." Mary said.

"Please, Miss Wendron, call me Roger. Tommy is not the only reason I came. I was wondering if you would be interested in going for a walk with me some evening?" asked Roger.

"Oh ... that would be nice. Thank you, Mr.—Roger," Mary replied, rather timidly.

"Would tomorrow evening be too soon? Weather permitting, that is? Since I'm on duty as soon as darkness settles, it would be early. If you'd like, I could walk you home from the orphanage."

"I would like that, Roger. I'm usually finished by four o'clock in the afternoon."

"I will be there, Miss Wendron."

"Please, call me Mary."

CHAPTER 11

Winnie was helping Tessa clean up the breakfast clutter when a dish fell from her hands and shattered at her feet. Tessa jumped. Winnie started to cry, hiding her face in her apron.

"Now don't get all upset, our Winnie; it's only a dish. I'll help ye sweep it up," Tessa said calmly, heading for the broom.

"It's no' the dish, Cook. It's Tommy. Whatever will 'appen to 'im? I'm that worried, I am! It's been two days now."

"Well, it's no use worryin' when it's out of our 'ands, lass. Why don't ye take these scraps out to the 'ogs, and I'll clean up here. Try to clear yer 'ead while ye're out there."

No sooner did Winnie open the back door when in flew Tommy, grabbing Winnie and twirling her around. "I'm 'alf-starved, I am. What's to eat?"

Tessa gave him a big bear hug, sat him down at the table, and commenced preparing a plate of eggs and cold rashers. "Eat this, Tommy, then tell us all about it, lad."

Forgetting the hogs, Winnie dried her eyes, hugged Tommy from behind, and plopped down in the chair next to him. "We were so afraid for ye, Tommy. Didn't know if we'd ever see ye again."

"Well, 'ere I am, Winnie," he said as he washed down the last of a dry rasher with some juice. "I'm no worse off than when ye saw me last. Had a time of it, though. Saw me staring at the water, they did. Ain't no crime in that. Couldn't 'old me on nothin' else. Just asked me what I saw and who I saw."

"Who did you see, Tommy?" Winnie asked, hoping to hear news of Roger.

"Ain't sayin' names, Winnie. Lots of people were down there lootin' cargo and cudgelin' 'eads. It were a mess—blood all over." Tommy didn't mention the body floating at his feet. The thought of it gave him the shivers. "Saw 'em take one of Jock Hastings' men away afore they 'auled me off. That's all I know."

Tessa added a blueberry muffin to his plate and said, "Glad ye're 'ome, laddie. Maybe ye'll think twice next time ye feel like playing smuggler. That was quite a scare you 'ad."

"Hrumpf!" bellowed Tommy. "I ain't scared o' nothin' or nobody." Tessa and Winnie shook their heads as Tommy grabbed another muffin and stuffed it in his mouth.

Lundy sat dejectedly on a three-legged stool in front of Roger Hawker and his men. He had been questioned for over four hours with no food or water. He kept repeating over and over, "I ain't no snitch." He already sported a shiny black eye from Donny Brady, one of Roger's more enthusiastic interrogators. He was manhandled all the way to Bodmin Prison and thrown roughly into a damp, filthy cell with only a brick-sized hole far above his head for light. He was to remain there until the next assizes (inquests held periodically by the high court), where he would be put on trial for a number of questionable offenses.

Meanwhile, back at the Owler, Jock paced back and forth unable to settle into his normal routine. He had been distracted since the night of the raid. He refused his evening meals and told Sal to go to bed without him. His mind was on Lundy. Jock knew Lundy well enough to know he would not turn informer. He was uneasy about Lundy's treatment by the revenue men. He knew Donny Brady well, and there were others like him who were dangerous in their handling of prisoners and boasted of it. He had known men who lost their eyesight, and some their fingers, to the fiendish cruelty of men like Donny. Whistler had kept his distance since the raid. Jock knew Harry was frightened when he saw Lundy hauled away. This was the first time one of Jock's men was seized, and they were all feeling skittish. He knew Roger Hawker was coming to question him, as well as the rest of his crew. They needed to be ready.

CHAPTER 12

The children had always anticipated Christmas with much excitement. This year was no different. They had decorated the tops of the doors and windowsills with holly. Laughter filled the room as boys and girls alike sat at the dining room table frosting gingerbread cookies. Sarah ran around the table adding raisin eyes to each smiling face. The benefactors of Tremorna Orphanage had provided each child with a basket of goodies, which included a big, juicy orange and a small bag of nutmeats. Carols were sung by the fireplace, and Cook had made special treats for the occasion. The children were allowed to stay up late, playing with their new trinkets and enjoying each other's company.

The new year brought change at the orphanage. Sarah Lamb, at the age of five, was leaving her friends behind for a new life with a new family. Liza was in Sarah's room helping her into the brand new dress made by the seamstresses of Tremorna. Long ago, these women decided they would provide each orphan child with a new outfit to begin their new life. The rest of the townspeople joined in by furnishing shoes, stockings, and much-needed undergarments. Sara's dress was a deep pink with puffy sleeves and a collar of pure white lace. "You look beautiful," Liza sighed. "Like a little princess." Liza gave her a tearful hug. She would miss her friend, but wished her well.

Sarah twirled around when Pudgie whistled at her from the doorway. "Be careful, little Sarah. I might just come an' whisk ye away someday. We'll get married an' have lots of sweet little girls just like ye." Pudgie left and the girls fell back onto Sarah's bed in a fit of giggles.

Sister Therese almost knocked Sister Matias down in her rush to the Reverend Mother's office. Not bothering to knock, Sister Therese burst in on Sister Agnessa. Dawn had broken and matins had just concluded; this was her quiet time. "Heavens, what is it, Sister?"

"A baby, Reverend Mother! A baby!"

"Sit down and calm yourself, Sister. What is this all about? What baby?" Sister Agnessa asked, trying to remain composed.

Sister Therese sat on the edge of a chair for a second but couldn't control her excitement. She jumped up again and exclaimed, "I was walking back to my room just now, and there was a pounding on the door. I was afraid for a few seconds and thought I should come and get you first. Then I decided to open the door, and there it was! A baby! In a basket!"

By now Sister Agnessa was on her feet, demanding that Sister Therese take her to the baby. "I left it in my room and came to you straightaway, Reverend Mother."

Babies left on the doorsteps of orphanages were nothing new, but it was the first time it had happened since Sister Therese's arrival. It was understandable that she would become unsettled by this event, surmised Sister Agnessa. (Of course, the Reverend Mother did not know that, in her former life as Kerena Dugan, Sister Therese had done the exact same deed to save her own son from his father.) The Reverend Mother swept into the room just as the baby started to cry. It was clear to her, as she picked the infant up in her arms, that it was a newborn. Bundled in a pale yellow blanket, it looked up at the nun, and its lungs gave out a strong bellow. Sister Agnessa shushed the baby as she unwrapped it. Placing it on a nearby table, she noticed that a note clung to the blanket. It simply said "Emily." "Welcome to your new home, Emily," whispered Sister Therese.

"I am putting you in charge of Emily for now, Sister Therese. Keep her in your room. I will see what I can do about finding one of the women from town to nurse her as soon as possible." Closing the door behind her, the Reverend Mother looked back to see Sister Therese rocking little Emily to sleep.

Children and staff said their farewells to Sarah as she walked down the front lane to the waiting carriage. Standing between her new parents, Joel and Julia Carne, she turned and waved. Taking Julia's hand, she smiled up at Joel, her cheeks wet with tears. "You are a brave little girl, Sarah, to leave all of your friends here for a new life," assured Joel.

Julia squeezed Sarah's hand. "You and I are going to have such fun, Sarah! Come now, we must travel quite a distance and want to get home before dark." As the carriage drove away, Sister Agnessa bowed her head and thanked the dear Lord for finding such a good home for Sarah. She knew that the Carnes were a wealthy family and were well liked in their community. Sarah would not only be well taken care of, but she would be loved.

That night, Pudgie heard Liza crying softly. He knew she would miss Sarah most of all.

—•——o—O—o——•—

Smuggling activities had been put on hold since Lundy's imprisonment. A somber cloud settled over the Owler. The men drank to excess and stumbled home to their beds. Sal's efforts to liven things up a bit had only made things worse. Jock, however, couldn't let things stand as they were. He needed a plan. He would take on a new man for the time being. It couldn't be helped.

The next day, Jock put the word out that he was looking for a man to join his crew. Anyone interested was to come to the Owler and ask for Sal. Sal was a good judge of character, and Jock trusted her completely to make the best choice for a crewmate. She'd hired Lundy and Whistler and several other members of his crew.

A week passed. Sal was becoming discouraged. After talking to several men interested in joining Jock's gang, she found them all lacking. When a man named Jeremy Dugan walked into the Owler, Sal was on her guard. She'd heard of this man. She knew he had run with quite a rowdy band of smugglers until he had been caught receiving stolen contraband and sentenced to Bodmin Prison. She also knew that he had had many successful runs earlier and had a reputation of being startlingly ruthless. Jock wanted honest men on his crew—as honest as thieves can be between themselves. Sal would question Mr. Dugan to see if he would own up to his prison stay. If so, she'd take him on. Anyone could be arrested if they weren't careful. "Look at poor ol' Lundy," she thought. Jeremy would be a bit thin for Jock's liking, Sal thought, but he looked fit enough. When asked about his past, he did admit to spending nine years in Bodmin Prison. He seemed proud of it, and gleefully told Sal all about his cellmates' tales of murder, deceit, and revenge. He related that their stories only stirred his longing for his smuggling days, and he couldn't wait to "get me 'ands dirty again." A terrible mistake in his judgment had led to his imprisonment, he said. He knew better now.

—o—O—o—

Sister Matias and Winnie were cooing over little Emily when the Reverend Mother walked into the room with a young woman from the village. Her name was Priscilla Treet, and Sister Agnessa introduced her as the woman who was to nurse Emily. A bed had been moved into the nursery for Priscilla as she would be living at the orphanage for the foreseeable future. "Welcome, Mrs. Treet," Winnie and Sister Matias chimed at the same time.

"Please call me Prissy. It's nice to meet ye both. If ye'll excuse me, I'd like to get acquainted wi' the babe." As Prissy said this, Emily let out a loud wail. Prissy picked her up and sat in the rocking chair next to the crib. "I believe this little lady is tryin' to tell me somethin'." The sisters and Winnie took that as their cue to leave Prissy and the babe alone for the feeding.

As the Reverend Mother closed the door she said, "If there is anything you need, please let me know." Prissy simply nodded. She already had Emily at her breast.

Sister Agnessa went to inform Sister Therese of Prissy's arrival. She found her looking out the window of her bedroom, staring down at the orphanage playground. The Reverend Mother walked over to the window and looked down. There were no children outside as it had rained all night, and the grounds were puddled and muddy. As Sister

Therese had not moved from that spot nor said a word, Sister Agnessa quietly left the room. "She is a mystery," she thought to herself.

CHAPTER 13

Prissy Treet took her morning meal in the dining room with the children. She noticed that Liza was picking at her food and looking rather forlorn. "Ye look like ye just lost yer best friend, Liza," Prissy exclaimed.

Billy piped up with, "She did! She did! She's missin' our Tharah shomethin' awful, Mrs. Treet. Just mopes 'round all day long."

Even amongst the playful chatter of the other orphans, Liza was mourning the loss of Sarah's funny laugh and cheerful ways. "T'ain't the same 'round 'ere without 'er," Liza whispered.

Prissy felt sorry for the girl. She knew what it was like to feel lonely. She had no siblings and grew up in a sad old cottage with her miserable aunt. If it wasn't for her cat Brunhilda, Prissy would have had no one to talk to. When she was nineteen she was wed to their widowed neighbor, Silas Treet. He treated her well and helped her look after her aunt until she died. Fourteen years ago, Prissy gave birth to their first child, Charity. There were no brothers or sisters for Charity until a little over a year ago, when Silas and Prissy became parents once more. This time, they had a boy, Cedric. Charity was old enough to watch Cedric, and he was feeding from a bottle now. Prissy was free to earn some extra wages by becoming wet nurse to little Emily at the orphanage.

Prissy looked over at Liza's sad face and suddenly an idea came to her. "Liza, would ye like to 'elp me bathe the new baby?"

Liza's eyes widened as she sat up straight. "Me?"

"Yes, I sure could use yer 'elp." Prissy winked at Billy as Liza jumped up and followed her into the nursery.

Jock and his crew had been gone for over a week now, obtaining illegal kegs of French brandy and cases of tobacco at the port of St. Malo on the French coast. It was a longer route than to the Channel Islands but afforded a more sheltered area for smugglers. (Both the British and French watched the Channel Islands because they were the quickest way for smugglers to move goods.) Jeremy had never been involved in the bargaining for and transport of contraband. Jock thought it a good idea to have him learn this side of the business, even though he would be used mostly for wrecking ships and bludgeoning survivors. For now, he would be most useful in unloading the goods from the ships into smaller fishing boats. Because of Lundy's bad luck, Jock planned to drop the goods at Mullion Cove first. Once he knew the coast was clear, his men would reload and quietly row into Holly Bay.

On the trip back from the coast of France, Jeremy had a lot of time to ponder his situation. When first released from Bodmin Prison, he had gone back to his hovel in Polvenon. His son, Matthew, would have been 11 years old. He couldn't wait to see him. Kerena was another story. He didn't understand why he ever married her. They were different as chalk and cheese. Hopefully she hadn't turned his son into a blithering milksop! The way she smothered him, he wouldn't have been a bit surprised.

When he had arrived in Polvenon there had been no sign of either Kerena or his son. He had met the new "owners" of the cottage—squatters just like he, Kerena, and Matthew had been. They too, had no deed to the property or legal right to be there. He moved on. Asking around the village had not provided any clues to the whereabouts of his wife and son. He even tried to threaten Doc Hayle without success. How long had they been gone? Where did they go? He vowed he would find them someday, and when he did, he would take Matthew and leave Kerena destitute. She deserved it.

CHAPTER 14

The year flew by quickly. Emily was almost a year old, had started on soft foods, and was being bottle-fed. Prissy's services were no longer required, but she liked to stop in now and then to see how the infant was doing. Sister Therese and Liza vied for Emily's attention, while Tommy steered clear of her as he "don' like bawling babies."

Christmas was approaching, and Father Cotter sat down with the children in the makeshift schoolroom to tell them the story of the birth of Jesus. "Once the holy family arrived in Bethlehem, they found that there was no room in the inn for them to stay. The only place the innkeeper could offer was a lowly stable."

Pudgie piped up. "Why didn' they kick someone outta the inn to make room? Didn' they know how important that baby was gonna be?"

"Not right away, Pudgie. No one knew how special that baby was until the wise men came to the stable. An angel had appeared to them and told them where to find Jesus. They were told that the baby Jesus had come to save sinners like you and me. Then the good news was spread far and wide. That is what Christmas is all about."

Father Cotter stood and shouted, "Happy Christmas, children!"

Liza had been standing at the back of the schoolroom holding Emily in her arms. Emily let out a shriek and Tommy hollered over the noise, "Did Jesus cry as loud as our Emily?" At that everyone laughed, and poor Emily cried even louder.

On his way home, Father Cotter spied Mary Wendron and Roger Hawker walking hand in hand along the cliff path. He was happy for Mary. She deserved someone like Roger—someone who walked the straight and narrow and would take good care of her. He sincerely hoped something good would come of their courtship.

Back at the rectory, Father Cotter wiped the sweat from his brow. Before dawn, Jock and his crew had dropped a "package" off to be stored in the cellars below. The priest was getting nervous. His home was being used more and more as a drop-off point ever since the last raid. He needed to have a talk with Jock. It had to stop. He was pretty sure there were eyes watching not only the rectory, but the churchyard as well.

Father Cotter was not the only one who had observed Mary and Roger walking together. Winnie had also spotted them going past the orphanage gardens when she had brought the washtubs outside to empty them. She seethed at the sight. Mary was not good enough for Roger. Winnie was almost 14 now and had more than a fleeting interest in Roger. "What does he see in her?" Winnie wondered. "She's mousy and plain! She's just a lowly housekeeper!" Winnie reminded herself that she, too, held a rather humble position as kitchen help. Sighing heavily, she lugged the slop buckets in through the back door.

—o—O—o—

It seemed to Tommy that Jock was keeping him at bay since the raid. Jock had told Tommy when he first took him on that he was never to come to the Owler. He was to wait until Jock contacted him. It had been several months now, and Tommy was getting itchy.

He had heard that the St.Malo run went smoothly and that the men were yet again lying low. Sitting near the edge of the cliff, Tommy was whittling away and thinking about Lundy. He hadn't heard yet how long Lundy's sentence would be. He was thinking about what it would be like to be transported to the wilds of Australia and assigned hard labor there. He hoped it wouldn't come to that.

"Hello, Tommy," Sister Matias spoke softly so as not to scare him off the edge of the cliff. She sat down next to him and watched his expertise at whittling. "Where did you learn how to do that, Tommy?"

"It was Nathan showed me 'ow. Afore 'e left 'e gave me 'is knife. Said 'e wouldn't be needin' it as the people who took 'im are rich an' they'll buy 'im a nice new one."

Nathan was an older boy who was adopted into the Tregildry family. They owned a rather lucrative pub in Truro, and although Sister Matias did not consider the family "rich" by any means, they were fairly well off. Nathan was fortunate to have the opportunity to become a part of their close-knit family.

"Would you whittle something for me, Tommy?"

"Sure thing! What would ye like? I can't whittle animals like Nathan could, but I can carve up a nice boat for ye."

"Oh, anything at all, Tommy. I will cherish it because you made it for me, no matter what it is." She leaned over and gave him a peck on the cheek. "I have to go now. Enjoy yourself, and be careful near the cliff."

Sister Matias walked away leaving Tommy blushing deeply, but with a smile on his grubby face.

Winnie was in the gardens walking little Emily in her pram. Her thoughts were all of Roger. She knew that he had feelings for Mary Wendron. "Somehow I have to get him to notice me. But how?" she wondered. She strolled up to the stone bench near the edge of the rose garden and sat down. She noticed Tommy coming down from the cliff path and waved. A plan started to form in her devious mind. She motioned for Tommy to come and sit with her.

"Whatcha got there, Tommy?"

"A boat—the beginnin' of one anyway." Tommy hoped that his rosy cheeks had faded by now. Winnie would tease him to no end if she sensed his embarrassment at being kissed by Sister Matias. Emily was sleeping peacefully, and Tommy had a chance to get a good look at her. "Sure is a beaut, eh?"

"Yes, she is. Tommy, would ye do a favor for me?"

"Sure thing. Anything fer ye!"

"Well, this has to be our secret. Ye can't tell anyone." Winnie knew Tommy's feelings for her and knew he wouldn't betray her. "I want you to find Roger and let him know that Mary wants to meet him tonight on the cliff path. Don't tell him I told you. It's to sound as if ye are givin' 'im the message from Mary. Can you do that, Tommy?"

Asking no questions, Tommy hollered, "Sure can!" as he ran up the foot path, leaving his little boat behind.

Later that day, when Mary walked through the kitchen to empty her bucket and get fresh water, Winnie whispered loudly to Cook so Mary would be sure to hear. "Roger wants me to meet 'im tonight on the cliff path."

Meanwhile, preparations were being made for Emily's first birthday. The girls were decorating the dining room with pretty pink ribbons and bows tied to each chair. Sister Matias had picked fresh peonies and placed them in the middle of the table. Sister Agnessa had just entered the room, admiring their handiwork, when Liza ran in waving a letter. "It's from our Sarah!" She handed it to Sister Agnessa, who began to skim Sarah's missive. Sarah's scratching was barely legible.

The Reverend Mother told the children that Sarah loved her new home. "She says she is living in Cadgwith and has an older brother whose name is Andrew. She has a room twice as large as the one she had here. Her window looks out onto the cove. It reminds her of Holly Bay. She says she misses everyone but is very happy. She sends her love to all." Sister Agnessa passed the last page of the letter around, as Sarah had drawn a picture of her new kitty, Simon.

Liza left the room feeling dejected. There was no reference to her in Sarah's letter. A tap on her shoulder turned her around. "Liza dear, I didn't want the others to hear, so I purposely skipped reading part of her letter. She wanted you to know that she misses you the most and hopes one day you could come for a visit."

"Oh, Sister! Could I visit Sarah?"

"We'll see. Right now, just be happy that she loves you and misses you dearly. You always were her favorite, you know."

The Reverend Mother walked away, and right then and there Liza made a promise to God: she would pray harder than she ever had before if only He would let her see Sarah again.

That evening, Roger waited for Mary to come. He turned when he heard footsteps, but it was only Winnie coming down the path toward him. Just as she reached him, she "accidentally" stumbled—right into his arms! Thanking him profusely for catching her, she clung to him with her arms wrapped around his neck and kissed his cheek. She saw Mary coming up the path from the other direction and knew that she had seen the kiss. Shocked, Mary turned and ran home blinded by her tears.

CHAPTER 15

Jeremy had been living in one of the upstairs rooms in the Owler Pub. In his free time, he had taken to wandering the streets of Tremorna and neighboring towns in search of any news of Kerena and Matthew. Once, he thought he spied his wife coming out of a shop on the main street of a town a few miles from Polvenon, but it wasn't she. He had hoped that Matthew looked enough like either Kerena or himself so that he'd recognize him when he saw him. When he closed his eyes, he pictured him to look just like Kerena, who, despite her annoying ways, was a real beauty at one time. He remembered her shiny ebony curls and her deep brown eyes. After Matthew was born, she had let herself go. Her hair had become dull and streaked with gray, her eyes lifeless. She used to laugh a lot but, for some reason, had lost her smile. He never did understand her. He put food on the table and made sure they had a roof over their heads. Still, it hadn't been enough. He had been glad to turn his back on her. If it weren't for Matthew, he wouldn't care if he ever saw her again.

—o—O—o—

It was Sunday. Pudgie and Billy were outside practicing for their next cricket match. The bats were ancient, but there was no money for replacements. There were not enough boys at the orphanage to make up two official-sized teams, so they made do with two teams of seven players each. Billy was too clumsy to be a very good player, so Pudgie always made sure he was on Billy's team to make up the deficit with his long legs. Liza was sitting on the sidelines pouting because they wouldn't let girls play. Winnie was there cheering them on. It was a beautiful day; the sunlight glittered on the calm water of the cove. Tommy was watching the families out in rowboats with their picnic baskets and fishing poles enjoying the weather.

Prissy, her son Cedric, Sister Therese, and Emily were sitting on a blanket watching the practice game. Fairly often now, when Prissy came to visit Emily, she brought Cedric. Emily's face lit up whenever she saw him. They were both at the crawling stage, needing constant supervision. No one seemed to notice that Sister Therese kept her eyes glued to Tommy as he played. He looked nothing like his father. "Actually, he doesn't resemble me either," she thought. She had never seen her father but had been told by her mother that he had had red hair and a light complexion. He would be hard to spot if Jeremy ever came looking, and for that she was thankful.

Crack! Pudgie hit a ball so hard that everyone ducked, not knowing where it would land. It fell at the feet of Mary, who was just coming from the orphanage. She threw it to Tommy as Winnie waved her over to join them. Mary ignored her and walked down the lane toward home. Cook sat down next to Winnie and exclaimed, "Now I wonder what could be eatin' our Mary."

Tommy piped in, "Yeah, I wonder ..." as they both turned their eyes toward Winnie.

Jock and Sal had been plotting all morning. Plans were brewing for another run. They were arguing about whether or not it was safe to use Tommy as a signal again. It had been quiet since Lundy's capture, and Tommy had lain low as directed. Jock thought it was time, but Sal had her doubts. "Don' ye think 'awker and 'is men are watching 'im?"

"Not so much anymore, Sal. They 'ave too many irons in the fire. The gangs from Polvenon and Bodmin are startin' to use the Pentruth port to unload their wares. 'Awker's cronies are elsewhere, so I say we risk it." Jock, observing carefully, had discovered a weak point in the chain of patrols guarding this section of the Cornish coast. Having completed this particular run successfully many times before, the time of their arrival in Holly Bay could be depended upon with some certainty. Tommy would be given the estimated time, and they could await his signal. "If it all goes bad, we can always sink the goods." The task of retrieving and landing the contraband later would be left to local men. They had intimate knowledge of the routine of the revenue men, and they knew the lay of the land beneath the coastal waters as well.

"Ye can do this route wi' yer eyes closed." Sal agreed. "Will ye be leavin' Jeremy behind this time then?"

"Aye. 'E can be second signal to Tommy, just in case. 'E's proven 'imself at sea, but 'e's best on land."

After cricket practice, Tommy was sitting at the edge of the playing field whittling on the boat he was working on the day before. A shadow fell over him. He hoped it wasn't Winnie. He felt bad about his part in deceiving Mr. Hawker like that. If he'd known what Winnie was up to, he may not have done what she'd asked. Still, Mr. Hawker was a revenue man. Tommy looked up when the shadow disappeared, and Jeremy Dugan sat down next to him.

"Looks like we've got a whittler in the making," Jeremy declared as he took the wood from Tommy and examined it closely. "That's fine work, lad. I used to whittle a bit meself. Me da taught me." Jeremy looked wistfully at the boy. "I'm hopin' someday to pass that skill on to me own son." Jeremy handed the boat back to Tommy. "Me name's Jeremy, by the way."

"Tommy."

"Well, Tommy, it's nice to meet ye." Jeremy stood up to walk away but turned, leaned toward Tommy and whispered, "Say ... are you the lad who does the signaling from the orphanage window?"

Tommy's eyes grew large, and he quickly turned his head away. "I don' do no signalin' from no window."

"Well ... Jock's hired me on, and I heard about the light from the window. Must be someone there doin' it."

Tommy's face rapidly colored. "Well, keep that to yersel' will ya?" he whispered harshly.

Chuckling to himself, Jeremy walked away. "That boy has spunk. I like that! I'll bet 'e didn't stay at 'is ma's teats for long!"

Sister Therese had been looking out the window watching Tommy. She jumped back in shock when she saw a man sit down next to him. She couldn't tell from the window if she knew the man or not, but a feeling of dread fell over her.

CHAPTER 16

That evening, Roger knocked on Mary's cottage door. He was worried that she or her mother had taken ill. What other explanation would there be for Mary to ask him to meet her last night and then not show up? Mary's mother answered the door. "Not too sure our Mary wants to see ye right now."

Evidently Mary's mother knew who Roger was even though they had never met. Assuming his uniform had given him away, he gave a slight bow. He told her that he was worried that something was wrong as Mary didn't meet him last night. "Oh, aye, somethin's wrong. Got yer fingers in too many pies, I'd say!"

She was about to shut the door in his face when Mary appeared behind her. "I'll talk to 'im, Mum. Would ye give us some privacy?"

"If it's privacy ye need, go out to the back garden. This 'ouse be tiny, and I'd 'ear every word no matter where I be." She shooed them out the door before Roger could say another word.

As they walked along the path to the garden, Mary would not look at him. She walked slightly ahead. She hadn't said a word. Confused, Roger didn't know what to say. He wanted to ask her what happened last night, but she seemed so cold and distant. "Mary … I—"

Mary swung around and faced him. "Why are you here, Roger? I think you made it clear last night where I stand. Please don't make it more difficult. Just go."

"Mary … I don't understand. It was you who sent the message for me to meet you on the cliff path last night. I stayed there a long time until I realized you weren't coming."

"I did no such thing! What message?"

"Tommy came to tell me that you wanted to meet me."

"I'm confused, Roger. I never sent a message to Tommy. I wouldn't involve him in anything so trifling." Tears started to flow. "I—I saw you kissing Winnie. Why would you do that?"

Things were becoming clear to Roger as he thought back to the incident with Winnie. Winnie put Tommy up to this! "Mary, Winnie tripped on the cliff path and fell into me. Now I'm thinking it was done on purpose. Don't you see? She wanted you to see us together." Roger had known for a long time now that Winnie had been a bit infatuated with him, but he never thought she would take it this far.

After hearing Roger's suspicions about Winnie's deceptive plot, Mary dried her tears and smiled up at him. "I've been a fool."

Roger took her in his arms. "Yes you have, Mary, for thinking that I could ever have feelings for anyone but you." He held her close and tenderly kissed the top of her head. Then, holding her at arm's length and looking into her eyes, he spoke slowly and surely. "I will have a talk with Winnie next time I see her. I will make it clear where my feelings lie. I love you, Mary." Right then and there, he knelt on the garden path and, in the middle of the crickets singing and the frogs croaking, asked her to marry him.

Sister Therese could not get the picture of her son "Tommy" and that man out of her thoughts. Why were they sitting together? Granted, she only saw the back of the stranger, but when he stood and started to walk away, he reminded her so much of Jeremy. She hadn't realized it, but it had already been over nine years since she'd seen her husband. She remembered the words of the drunken men at the Water's Edge Pub: "Nine years 'e got!"

"Oh my God!" she thought. "It can't be! Can he have found us? But how?" She knew she needed to keep a cool head for Matthew's sake as well as her own. She had been so careful not to disclose her plan to hide Matthew to anyone. She had covered her tracks well—at least she thought she had. She had to find out more about this strange man without being too obvious. If it was indeed Jeremy, she had to come up with a new plan—and quickly!

Roger spotted Tommy running toward the cove. He followed him. When he reached Tommy, he grabbed him by the arm and swung him around. "Not so fast, young lad. I have to talk to you."

"Huh? Wha' 'bout?" Tommy asked, his eyes shifting back and forth. He hoped no one would see him talking to the revenue man.

"That message you gave me the other day from Mary. Did someone put you up to that?"

Tommy wriggled out of Roger's grasp. "Wha' d' ye mean?"

"I mean that message didn't come from Mary, did it?"

Wanting to make a run for it but knowing it wouldn't help his situation, Tommy just shrugged.

"You don't have to tell me, Tommy. I know it was Winnie. What I want to know is why you agreed when you knew it would hurt Mary."

"I like Mary! I like our Winnie too! 'Sides, I didn't know wha' Winnie was up to 'cause I didn't ask. I did think it strange though. I just did it wi'out thinkin' why.

"You are right, Tommy. You didn't think. Winnie hurt Mary's feelings, and you were a part of that."

Roger hoped that he got through to Tommy, but he highly doubted it. "Now ... tell me where you are going in such a hurry."

"Geez, can't a chap just have a go wi'out all the questions?" And off he went, faster than a jackrabbit. Roger chuckled to himself as he walked toward the orphanage and an uncomfortable confrontation with Winnie.

CHAPTER 17

Jock and his crew had been gone close on a fortnight. Awaiting Tommy's signal, they sat in the pitch dark, their faces frosty and their lips blue. Whistler shivered and stomped his feet. " 'Tisss a cold one, eh? 'Nough to freeeeze me eyeballssss open!"

Jock agreed it was a bitter cold night, but he wasn't going to gripe. He had another successful run under his belt, and that's all that mattered. He did miss Lundy though. Before they had left, he had overheard some of the preventive men talking near the waterfront. "Those royalist bastards!" he thought. Evidently Lundy got seven years in the London prison. Better for Lundy had he been transported to New South Wales. At least he would have been working outdoors and not stuck in some rotten, rat-infested cell in the bowels of Newgate.

Jock looked up and saw Tommy's signal. They slowly rowed to shore and Jeremy was waiting there to unload. The goods were brought through the dimly lit tunnel into the cellars of the orphanage. When all the crates were stacked, the men sat on them to rest. Whistler grabbed a bottle of rum to toast another lucrative venture.

Meanwhile, Tommy sneaked back to his bedroom. He breathed a sigh of relief. He was beat and wanted nothing more than to sleep, but as he turned toward his bed, there was Pudgie. "Tommy. Where ya been?"

"Geez, Pudge! Ye scared the bloomin' shite outta me!"

"Didn' them nuns teach you nothin', Tommy? It's no' nice to swear."

Tommy threw a pillow at him. "Why are ye ' ere?"

"Answer me question first."

"It's nonna yer business. Now leave me be."

" 'Tis my business when ye wake me up all hours of the night wi' yer traipsin' in and out, and none too softly, I might add."

"Sorry, Pudge. Won' 'appen again."

"Oh, I think it will. I followed you tonight. Saw ye go up to the top rooms where we aren't allowed. Wha' ye got up there, eh? Or should I say, who?"

Tommy was getting tired of these questions. "Yeah! I got me a girl! We go up there to be alone, so leave be. I'm warnin' ye!"

"Calm down, Tommy. Just curious, tha's all. Didn't know ye had it in ye." Pudgie clapped him on the back, winked, and strolled out of the room.

Tommy sat down heavily on his bed. "That was close!" he thought. He hadn't realized anyone had noticed him come and go. It was usually so late that he assumed everyone had been fast asleep by then. Kicking off his noisy shoes, he scowled at them. "It's all yer fault! Next time ye won' be joinin' me. Go barefoot from now on, I will!"

Emily was nearly two years old and getting into mischief at every turn. Walking with a cute waddle, she followed Billy around like a shadow. "Biddy, Biddy!" she would call out whenever she spotted him. "Biddy" enjoyed the attention. He played little games with her—her favorite being hide-and-seek. She would squeal whenever Billy found her. She tended to hide in the same spot over and over, making it rather boring for Billy, but he feigned exuberant surprise at finding her anyway. She giggled and clapped her hands wildly every time. Many afternoons found them cuddled together in the big, overstuffed chair by the fireside. Billy read nursery rhymes from a big Mother Goose book while Emily's wondering gaze followed the pictures on each page. When Emily would doze, Billy would close his eyes too. Many times Cook had to wake them for the evening meal.

It was on just such a lazy afternoon that there came a loud pounding on the orphanage door. "Mercy!" cried Liza and jumped up from her jigsaw puzzle to answer it. There stood the most amazingly beautiful man Liza had ever seen! Waves of coppery hair fell to his shoulders, and sea green eyes sparkled as he smiled down at her.

"Good afternoon, miss. Might the Reverend Mother be available?"

Forgetting her manners, Liza closed the door and ran to get Sister Agnessa. When Sister opened the door, the man bowed. "How do you do? Are you the Reverend Mother?"

For a moment even Sister Agnessa seemed flustered by his good looks. "Er, yes I am. You wanted to speak to me, Mr.? ..."

"Monroe, Sister—Drew Monroe. I hope I am not disturbing you. I just need a moment of your time."

"Of course, Mr. Monroe. Please come in." She led him into a room off the entrance, and they sat down across from one another. "Now what is this all about? Is there something I can help you with?"

"I hope so, Sister. You see, my brother Drake went missing a few years ago."

"Oh, how awful for you!"

"Yes. I have been searching for him ever since. My family lives in Polvenon, and that is where he was last seen. I have gone door-to-door in our village, and no one has any idea of his whereabouts. I have expanded my search to all the neighboring towns. I am wondering, Sister, if you've seen a man in the area who fits my description, for he looks remarkably similar to me."

The Reverend Mother knew with absolute certainty that she had never seen a man who was anywhere nearly as handsome as this man sitting in front of her. "No. I am certain that I have not. However, many of the sisters here, as well as the children, have had more dealings with the outside world than I. They may have seen him. If you'd like, you could go around to the back gardens. The children who work in them should be out there weeding or harvesting. Some of our sisters should be there also and may be of some assistance to you."

As they stood, Drew Monroe took Sister Agnessa's hand in his. "You have been most kind. Thank you for taking the time to see me, Sister."

As he left to go around the orphanage to the gardens, the Reverend Mother watched him. "He reminds me of Jock when he was younger." Closing the door, she remembered how infatuated she was at the time. "Yes, he was quite handsome, indeed!"

Winnie was still reeling from Roger's stern rebuke and the news that he and Mary would be wed next spring. She didn't even notice that she'd been scratched mercilessly by thorns as she cut the best of the blush roses for a dining room table centerpiece. Liza was crawling around Winnie trying to reach the weeds closest to the bushes when a booming voice called, "Hello!"

Winnie's head swerved and Liza's popped up when they saw a man walking toward them. They liked what they saw. Winnie seemed to forget all about Roger and began to flirt outrageously with him. "Well now, who might ye be, sir? Did ye come to admire these beauties?"

"Name's Drew Monroe, miss. And yes, they are lovely. But they are not why I've come."

"Monroe … why does tha' name ring a bell?" Liza asked as she sauntered up to Drew.

Drew's face brightened. "Ye know my brother, Drake, perhaps?"

"No. Wait … isn't 'e the one who disappeared a while back? Yes! And at the same time, a woman from Polvenon, too, I believe. Tha's yer brother?"

Drew came back down to earth with a thud. "Yes, he is my brother, and I am looking for him. My search has been unsuccessful thus far. Have either of you seen anyone in this area who looks a lot like me?"

Liza's sad expression told him the answer was no. Winnie laughed unfeelingly and said, "I'd 'ave remembered if I 'ad." Ignoring her crassness, Drew thanked them both and moved on.

At the other end of a sprawling raspberry patch, Drew spied a nun picking fruit alongside a young boy. Their baskets were overflowing. "Excuse me, Sister. The Reverend Mother sent me to the gardens in the hope that you might be able to help me."

Sister Matias and Tommy listened to the man's plight, and then the nun spoke. "I'm sorry. I have not seen any strange men in the area. I wish you well in your search." Tommy grew thoughtful. He remembered talking to the newest member of Jock's crew a while back but couldn't remember his name. He knew that it wasn't Drake as he certainly did not look anything like the man standing in front of him.

As Drew was leaving the grounds, Winnie sidled up to him. "I can 'elp ye look. I'll keep me eye out for 'im. Stop by again soon, and just maybe I'll 'ave somethin' to report. Don't look so discouraged. 'E may turn up sooner than ye think."

CHAPTER 18

Another year had gone by, and Sister Therese thanked God every day that there had been no news of Jeremy. She hadn't seen the man anywhere in the vicinity. She wouldn't go near the cove for fear the man she had seen with Tommy was indeed Jeremy and might recognize her. She was filled with anguish. There were so many times she wanted to reveal her true identity to the Reverend Mother. Shame and fear kept her from confessing.

In a moment of weakness she had spoken with Pudgie and asked him to keep an eye on Tommy. He was to let her know if he noticed anything about Tommy's activities that might lead to trouble. She knew it was a risk, but she was desperate. Pudgie had never questioned why. Instead, he had told her that Tommy "has a girlfriend" he wasn't telling anyone about and "meets her late at night." Sister Therese herself had seen him come and go late at night several times, and she had been beside herself with worry. Meeting a girl was much better than the smuggling activities she had been afraid he was involved in. Hopefully it was only a boyish infatuation. Relief flooded over her.

Jock and his thugs had spent the last few days and nights aboard their boats fishing, spinning yarns, and enjoying smuggled rum and tasty fish pasties. They were, after all, fisherman by trade. Whistler had gotten pie-eyed and fell over the side of his pilchard boat. Jeremy had hauled him back in, laughing and pounding him on the back so hard that he'd lost his balance and fell in yet again. Eventually Jock had shouted, "Enough of yer tomfoolery, lads. I've somethin' to say, an' I want ye to listen good. Ye've all done me proud these last few runs." Mugs were raised, and boisterous cheers went up from his crew, each congratulating the other on a job well done.

Jock shouted above the clamor. "I said listen good! We've got our biggest run yet to come. Next month, we sail for Calais." Yet another cheer went up, as they knew that this was a major source of contraband brandy. This trip would most likely prove to be their most profitable. "We've got to be ready. Likely there'll be customs an' excise cutters tryin' to stop us. We all know the king's crews are a bunch of simpletons who'd run from their own shadows, 'specially out at sea where their skills are poor at best." Jock knew there were also fearless revenue crews using the element of surprise to their advantage. He chose not to mention those.

Jock told his men that it would take several weeks to work out all the connection points and signals between the larger ships and their smaller vessels. "We'll meet again in a month's time. In the meantime, keep yer ears and eyes open an' report anythin' suspicious to me. Now ... there's food and drink aplenty for ye all at the Owler. I say we go ashore and continue the merry-making there!" Mugs were lifted and a toast was made. "To the Owler!"

"To S-ssal!" Whistler cried as the lapping waves met him one more time.

Father Cotter was having his morning tea. His housekeeper, Jennie Martin, always laid a place for him at the kitchen table. She knew he enjoyed the view from the window there. "Good mornin', Father."

"Good morning, Jennie. Another dreary day today, eh?"

"Yes, Father. Not much to look at." A thick fog had rolled in and covered the coastline as far as the eye could see. The windows were streaked with moisture, and a damp chill filled the air. "I'll get a fire goin'. That'll be just the thin' to warm our bones."

"Thank you, Jennie." Father Cotter had more on his mind than his cold, old bones. Roger Hawker's men had been spotted in the churchyard last night searching fresh graves and disturbing the rest of the newly-laid souls. "I have to get to Jock soon and let him know I'm done with this business," he said to himself. He did enjoy a good stiff brandy, but lately it had come at too great a cost. He had lived in constant fear, dreading Jock's visits as well as Roger's.

Jennie interrupted his thoughts. "There ye are, Father. I've put yer Bible an' eyeglasses next to yer chair. A good day to stay in, I'd say."

"No, Jennie. Thank you, but I've got somewhere I've got to go first." Jennie sighed as he grabbed his tattered overcoat and his crooked walking stick, leaving the kitchen and blending into the heavy Cornish fog.

Winnie and Liza were making raspberry jam. Cook was trying the latest method of preserving jam by using wax to seal it in small, glazed earthenware. They had even enlisted Billy's help in measuring out the sugar for each batch. Mary swept through the kitchen several times, a smile on her face. Winnie did not acknowledge her, and Liza wondered what was up. They hadn't spoken one civil word to each other for months, and both were tight-lipped whenever Liza mentioned it. Cook just "tsk-tsked" about the kitchen, shaking her head and wondering when one of them would break this oppressive silence. She had tried to step in several times, but withering looks from both had kept her quiet ever since.

Suddenly, the sugar slipped from Billy's grip and covered the floor around him. "Oh no!" Billy groaned, suddenly looking sick.

Cook, hands on hips, took one look at Billy's face, shushed the giggles coming from the other end of the counter, and said, "It's okay, Billy. Plenty more sugar in the larder. You go and get another sack, and I'll get a broom. We'll 'ave this cleaned up in no time." The price of sugar was dear, but Cook didn't let on. Billy was a good lad and had taken quite a lot of bullying from Pudgie and Tommy lately. It was the first time he had offered to help out in the kitchen. She didn't want it to be his last.

Later in the afternoon, when the jam was cooling on the counter, Billy and Liza sat at the table having their tea and biscuits. Sister Hildegard entered quietly, quickly pulling Cook off to the side. "I don't want to alarm the children, Tessa, but we may have a case of something serious in one of my patients. Please prepare a poultice as soon as you can, and bring it to me in the infirmary."

"What do ye think 'tis, Sister?"

"Well, the poor child has had a runny nose and a sore throat for the past day or two, but now a cough has developed. There's a fever too, and I'm beside myself with worry. I fear it may be the whooping cough. God's wounds, it sounds horrible! The poor thing is having trouble catching her breath."

"I know just the thin', Sister. Leave it to me. My plaster of mustard and herbs should take care of it. Shouldn't take but a minute."

"I'll wait. I don't want anyone else near the infirmary until we know for sure it's not going to spread. Please keep this to yourself, Tessa—at least for now."

CHAPTER 19

A hush fell over the orphanage as news of poor Janie Tabbert spread. She was said to be "sick unto death." No one had been allowed to visit her with the exception of her caretaker, Sister Hildegard, and at times, Father Cotter. Her cough grew worse every day, and her fever was high—too high. Sister Hildegard was at the end of her rope. She wrung her hands as she watched every breath that Janie took. Poultices had no effect on her condition. The room was kept warm, and heavy quilts were piled onto the poor soul in the hope that her fever would break. A doctor was brought in to examine her, but he just shook his head and told them they had done all they could.

Soon the news of Janie's illness reached the townspeople. Fear ran rampant as they remembered the diphtheria epidemic that had occurred years before. One day Mr. Terwilliger, the area's tinker, was traveling through. He saw the panic on the faces of the townspeople. Asking one woman why, he was told of the "dying girl" at the orphanage and how people were afraid the illness might spread. He drove his horse and cart right up to the front door of the orphanage and rapped loudly. Sister Therese answered. Standing before her in his tattered hat and long, shabby coat, he was a sorry-looking but familiar sight.

"Oh, Mr. Terwilliger. How kind of you to come by. I am afraid we are in a bad way here and now is not the time—"

Mr. Terwilliger held up his hand to stop her. "Sister, I think I may be able to 'elp."

"Mr. Terwilliger, I really don't think there is anything on your cart that would help this little girl."

"No, not me, Sister. I know someone. She knows things, although she does 'ave strange ways. A mender of maladies, ye might say."

"I don't think ..."

"A blender of balms, she is."

"But we don't ..."

"A concocter of cures. A purveyor of potions an' all manner of elixirs." He paused, allowing this to sink in.

"Wait a minute," exclaimed Sister Hildegard, who had come into the foyer and had heard most of the conversation. "At this point, Sister Therese, I'm willing to try anything. If this woman can help in any way, I say we let her try."

"If you think that's best, Sister Hildegard," Sister Therese concurred, as she stepped back to let them work out the details.

"Right then! I'll bring ' er ' ere on the morrow. I'll tell ' er to bring ' er grindin' bowl, for the ' erbs ye know." Mr. Terwilliger bowed reverently and went on his way.

•——o—O—o—•

"… and I am telling you it's too dangerous!" Father Cotter exploded as Jock refused to see reason. "I won't risk it anymore! It's not worth it!"

"And I am telling you, Father, that you don't really have a choice in the matter." Jock kept his temper in check. He spoke calmly, yet firmly. "We will continue to use yer accommodations as we see fit. Ye get paid 'andsomely in the spirits ye do so crave. I would say we both benefit equally."

"Spirits be damned! Do ye not hear what I am saying? They will find us out, and all the spirits in the world won't help me then!" Father Cotter was tempted to smile at his own religious pun but thought better of it.

"I dare say, yer "spirits" do keep us safe, as we all know the graveyard be 'aunted." Jock bellowed, not shy about his joke.

"Ye won't be laughin' when we're sharin' a cell in Newgate!" Father Cotter hissed. He stomped out. It was no use. The priest was not getting through to Jock. He had a mind to turn himself and the whole lot of Jock's crew in to the revenue officer. "Might just get a lighter sentence," he thought, but then he shuddered, remembering the tales he'd heard about what thugs did to turncoats. Hadn't he heard about a priest who danced below the gibbet for "consorting in a devilish fashion" with revenue-evading smugglers? They hung the holy man just to prove to one and all that no one was above the law. Father Cotter shuddered again.

Liza was outside reading. Sister Therese had been watching her as she turned the pages of her book. She wondered if she was Tommy's girlfriend. It made sense. She was beautiful. Most of the boys seemed to have a little crush on her, but she kept to herself. If Liza had any clue as to their interest in her, she didn't let on. Sister Therese knew of her family background and thought it quite sad that her parents gave her away to the orphanage. She had so many brothers and sisters at home. She never had a chance to know any of them. She sat down next to Liza. "What are you reading, Liza?"

"A book of poetry by Mr. Wordsworth. Listen to this. 'My heart leaps up when I behold a rainbow in the sky ...' It's such a beautiful poem, isn't it?"

"I've never heard that one before. Have you ever written a poem, Liza?"

"Nay. Ye 'ave to be smart for that!"

"I'm not so sure about that. I think if you take a look at all the beauty around you, the words might just come to you. Try it sometime. You may be surprised."

Liza looked at her, eyes wide. "Do ye honestly think so?"

"Yes I do, Liza. You are a very smart girl—very creative too. You could probably do 'most anything you set your mind to."

After Sister Therese went on her way, Liza gazed around her and slowly took in the grassy headland—the trees in the orchard heavy with shiny red apples. For the first time, she looked at the ancient church in the distance as a thing of great loveliness. She walked over to the edge of the cliff path and admired with new eyes the magnificent estuary and wild coastline dotted with pink sea thrift and white campion. Red valerian and maidenhair ferns stood out among the grasses beneath the gnarly, bent larch trees.

Suddenly, all Liza wanted to do was run back to her room and begin to write of these things, and yes, maybe even set them to lines of poetry!

CHAPTER 20

The foreign woman Mr. Terwilliger brought to the orphanage stood before Sister Hildegard and the Reverend Mother. She was dressed in a colorful flowing skirt, wore scarves around her head, and had large, golden hoops hanging from her ears. She carried a large leather pouch with smaller bags attached to a belt around her waist.

"This be Maleva, Sisters—the woman I tol' ye 'bout who might 'elp the young lass."

The Reverend Mother stood there silently as Sister Hildegard took Maleva's hand and invited her in. "I'm so glad you've come, Maleva. Little Janie does not seem to be improving no matter what we try. Please come and see if there is anything you can do for her." As she led the way to the infirmary, Maleva took in their funny way of dress. She had never seen a nun up close and wondered at the significance of the wimple and habit. She stifled a titter as she followed them. Being a sort of caregiver herself, she had too much respect for the work they did to make fun of their clothing.

Upon entering the sickroom, Maleva gasped. The air was stagnant and overly warm. It almost made one dizzy. The first thing she did was to open the window sashes. "This girl needs fresh air! Take those quilts off 'er! Someone run a cool bath—quickly!"

Maleva laid her head on Janie's chest and listened to her labored breathing. "Prop 'er up a bit. It'll 'elp 'er breathe easier. Take me to yer kitchen. Hurry!" No one questioned this strange woman and her unorthodox ways. As Maleva entered the kitchen, she shooed Cook out of the way. She asked what Cook used to prepare the plaster. "Get me those same herbs an' boil some water." Maleva carefully measured each herb and added the mixture to the water making a strong tea. Maleva noticed that Cook looked puzzled. She reassured Tessa that she had used the correct herbs for the poultice. "Herbs are right but work better as tea."

Sister Hildegard assisted Maleva in getting the tea down Janie's throat. "Now what?" Sister asked.

Maleva sat in the nearest chair. "We wait."

"Is Janie going to die?"

"No. She's got the hacking cough, but it's no' deadly."

"Is it catching, miss?"

"Aye, sad to say. Keep her apart from the others for at least a fortnight. If ye see any others sick in the same way, mix up the herbs and give it to 'em right away. They'll stop 'em from gettin' worse. Keep 'em apart if ye don't want it to spread."

The next morning the doctor came to check on Janie. He noticed that her color was much better. She was sleeping soundly, her breathing easier. Sister Hildegard told him of the strange woman's visit and what she had done for Janie. He nodded. "I've learned never to question the power of the gypsies, Sister. I've even consulted them in rare cases, as their knowledge of medicines and herbs is astounding. Most doctors scoff at their methods, but I've seen them perform miracles." He looked down at Janie. "I do believe she's one of those miracles."

Sister Therese knocked on the Reverend Mother's door. "Yes, Sister, what is it?"

"There is a couple to see you about adopting an infant, Sister. They are waiting in my office. Shall I send them in?"

Sister Agnessa nodded. Normally she would be more enthusiastic about meeting eager-to-adopt couples, but she knew that at the moment there were no infants at the orphanage.

As Sister Therese was leading the couple through the dining room, little Emily ran right into the woman, almost knocking her over, sending her hat flying to the floor. Billy, hot on her heels, barreled into Emily, launching her into Mrs. Trescowe a second time. "Oh!" was all Emily could say. She clapped her hands over her mouth and stared at the couple. Finally remembering what she'd been taught about manners, Emily gave a little curtsy. With her head down, she meekly whispered, "I'm so sorry."

The woman looked at the little girl. Emily reminded her so much of her own dear sister at that age. "What is your name, dear?"

"Emily."

"How old are you, Emily?"

Emily proudly held up four fingers.

"Well, that is a very nice age, Emily. Do you like living here?"

"Yes'm. It's me 'ome."

"Well, Emily, it was nice to meet you."

"Yes'm," Emily replied, giving a quick curtsy and running out of the room. Billy took up the chase.

"What a delightful child," the man and his wife said almost in unison.

Sister Therese explained how Emily was left on their doorstep as a baby with no explanation given—just a note that said "Emily."

Reaching the Reverend Mother's study, Sister Therese introduced the couple as Mr. and Mrs. Elliot Trescowe. Sister Agnessa shook their hands and offered them a seat. "I understand that you are looking to adopt an infant." Elliot and his wife Norah nodded. "Unfortunately, at this time we do not have any infants available here. Perhaps Bodmin Orphanage may be able to help you."

Norah Trescowe couldn't get little Emily out of her thoughts. "May we have a few minutes alone, Reverend Mother?"

"Of course. Take your time. I've some things I need to attend to. I will be back shortly."

Liza was sitting alone, her nose in her handmade journal, writing furiously. "Hello, Miss Liza." Liza jumped and looked up to see Drew Monroe smiling down on her. Her heart skipped a beat. He was as handsome as she remembered. "I was passing through and thought I'd check again to see if anyone has seen my brother in the area."

"No, Mr. Monroe. No one tha' looks like you. Where you going next?"

"Thought I'd try the Bude area. Haven't been there yet, and it's not too far. Of course, he may have been hauled off and pressed into service by those thieving smugglers, but then his fiancé, Miss Margaret, would surely have turned up by now."

"Sit down, Mr. Monroe. Tell me all about the places you've been so far."

"The name's Drew, and I don't want to bore you."

"Oh, I wouldn't be bored at all—really. I love to hear about faraway places."

"Well, I haven't been that far away, but I could tell you of the places I've been since I last saw you."

"Please do, Drew."

As Drew regaled her with tales of the towns and villages he had visited in his search, Liza hung on every word. She would close her eyes and try to picture towns with breathtaking cathedrals and beautiful stone bridges. She would laugh at his stories of strange townspeople he'd met in cozy pubs and the scraggly animals that seemed drawn to him like a magnet.

Suddenly Drew was silent. She looked at him and saw that he was smiling at her. "You really are enjoying hearing of my travels?"

"Oh yes! Some days I am tempted to just leave here and go wherever the road takes me."

"Well I do believe, Miss Liza, that you have a bit of the gypsy in you. Do you think you're old enough to go off on your own?"

Liza tossed her head rather impudently, her raven hair cascading on her shoulders. "I do believe that when the time comes, I'll be able to 'andle meself quite nicely, thank you. I'll be fifteen in a few months, an' after that—who knows?" She lowered her eyes demurely and said slowly, "Although I most likely would fare better travelin' wi' a guide."

She raised her eyes to meet his, holding her breath expectantly. Drew gazed back. "You would make a very beautiful gypsy." He kissed the tip of her nose. "Next time I pass this way, I do hope that you haven't spread your wings just yet."

Winnie had been watching from the window, tears streaming down her cheeks. She'd lost Roger to Mary Wendron, and now, by the way Drew looked at Liza, she'd lost her chance with him too.

CHAPTER 21

"Thank you, Reverend Mother, for giving us some time to think," Elliot Trescowe said as Sister Agnessa returned to her office.

"Not at all. Adoption is not a thing to take lightly. Have you made a decision? Would you like me to give you the directions to the orphanage in Bodmin?"

Norah cleared her throat. "Actually, Sister, we've decided that unless she is already spoken for, we'd love to give that lovely little girl we just met in the dining room a good home—Emily, her name is, I think. Can you tell us more about her?"

The Reverend Mother was surprised. She paused to think. The Trescowes were a well-known family in Polvenon. They ran the Rumford Inn, a most respectable establishment. Any child would be very lucky to have them as parents. But ... they came here looking for an infant. Suddenly they wanted to adopt a four-year-old girl. Should she grant their spur-of-the-moment wish to adopt Emily? If she did, would this placement fail because of the Trescowes' initial desire for an infant? What if Emily disappointed them? Could Emily's heart heal if it didn't work out?

The pause lengthened. Finally the Reverend Mother spoke. "Mr. and Mrs. Trescowe, it is our goal here to ensure that each child in our care is adopted into a warm and loving home. Emily was left on our doorstep when she was an infant. All we know about her is her first name. She has been very happy here. May I ask why you have taken an interest in her? Earlier, Sister Therese had informed me of your request for an infant. Emily is a wonderful little girl, but she is not what you were looking for, is she? What has made you change your mind?"

Norah Trescowe had tears in her eyes as she answered. "I lost my dear sister about five years ago, Reverend Mother. It broke my heart. She was the light of my life. One day she just disappeared. There has been no word of her since."

As Norah wiped the tears from her face, Elliot continued, "You see, Sister, your little Emily reminds us so much of Norah's sister. We know that Emily cannot replace Margaret in our hearts, nor would we want her to, but she could fill an emptiness that we've long felt. Norah and I saw her spunk and her playfulness earlier. I think we fell in love with her the first time she bumped into my wife. And then she bumped again!" Sister Agnessa nodded, smiling. "We need her, Sister, and she needs us. Please consider letting us adopt her."

Their tearful pleas melted the Reverend Mother's heart. Clearing her throat, she stood and took Norah's hand in hers. "I will have the papers drawn up for you to sign. We will need a little time to help Emily absorb this wonderful news and get her ready for her new home. Come back in a week's time. I am sure Emily will be ready."

Daniel, the orphanage groundskeeper, was called to the Reverend Mother's office. "I have a few errands for you to run, Daniel. Would you be able to take Sister Therese with you? She is in need of supplies for the main office."

"Aye, Sister. It'd be a pleasure. When will Sister Therese be ready?"

"I'm ready now, Daniel!" Sister Therese sailed into the room. She loved these outings but rarely went, still afraid someone might recognize her. However, there were items she really needed to purchase, and she felt much safer with Daniel as her companion.

Ink and paper were at the top of her list, but she couldn't wait to browse through all of the wonderful shops lining the main street of Tremorna. The confectionary was her favorite. They had everything from cakes and candies to sweetmeats and tarts. She purchased a lemon tart for herself, and on a whim she bought a small bag of wrapped taffy, the latest rage—a chewy candy made of molasses. She stepped out of the shop, on her way to the stationer, when she dropped her bag of taffy. Candy flew in all directions. As she stooped down to gather it up, a man walked up to her. "Need 'elp, Sister?"

Still looking down, she said, "Yes, that would be nice." Then smiling and raising her head, she intended to thank him. In what seemed only a second, her smile froze and her eyes widened in confusion and fear. Her heart stopped and she felt the hair on the back of her neck stand. Gulping for breath, she nodded in his direction and stumbled off. The stranger stood there for a minute. Jeremy hadn't seen Kerena in over 14 years, but he could have sworn that nun looked just like her!

On the way home, Daniel tried to make small talk with Sister Therese, but she just looked straight ahead. "Ye don' look so well, Sister. Maybe ye ate too much candy." Sister Therese was trembling inside and hoped it didn't show. Beads of sweat greased her brow and the back of her neck. Daniel stole a sidelong glance at her, then increased the horse's speed. He didn't relish having a sick nun on his hands and was glad when they made the turn into the orphanage lane.

Thankfully no one was in the foyer, and she was able to make it to her room without speaking to anyone. She grabbed the chamber pot and retched profusely. She was dizzy. Laying back on her bed, her breath in uneven spasms, she panicked. The room closed in on her. She needed air. She ran blindly to the rose gardens and fell to the ground sobbing until she thought her heart would stop again. She rolled onto her back and gazed at the late afternoon sky. Her mind moved slowly with the drifting clouds. Staring numbly at the stripes of lavender and peach etched across the horizon, her nerves began to settle. She told herself it couldn't have been Jeremy. He would have grabbed her and demanded to know where Matthew was. Instead, he just stood there while she walked away. No. It couldn't have been he.

CHAPTER 22

Emily walked hand-in-hand with Sister Matias to the Reverend Mother's office. She had been told of the Trescowes wanting to make a home for her. "You mean the lady I bumped into wants to be my new mommy?"

"Yes, Emily. Mr. and Mrs. Trescowe have asked for you specially. They have a lovely inn right near the water. They tell me there's a beautiful view from your bedroom window, and—"

"Will there be bars on the windows like here?"

"No. Of that you can be sure."

"But I won't know anybody there." She looked up at Sister Matias and asked, "Could Billy come along?"

The Reverend Mother heard Emily as they walked into the room. "Emily, come sit down. I'm afraid Billy can't come with you, but I'm told they have a young housekeeper. I'm sure she'll be happy to meet you. Their cook, Tudy, is our cook's twin sister, so it will be just like having Tessa there with you."

Emily was silent. Then she looked at Sister Agnessa and said, "You mean I'll have a real family?"

"You certainly will, Emily. Mr. and Mrs. Trescowe told me that they fell in love with you the minute they saw you. They will be here to see you again tomorrow and possibly take you home with them. Would you like that?"

A smile spread across Emily's face. "Yes, please."

Sister Matias had informed the other children of the possibility of Emily getting a real home. They had scurried about for goodbye presents in case it would really come true. As seldom as folks came to adopt, the children had still experienced disappointment when prospective parents had changed their minds and left the children behind.

Not wanting to get Emily's hopes up too high, Sister Matias had told her they could pack her satchel when it was time to go. Besides the few clothes she owned, she would take these gifts from her friends:

- two slightly crushed wildflowers;

- an oddly shaped stone ("I think it's magic," said Janie);

- a piece of bright red ribbon with tattered ends;

- a paper heart; and

- a gift from Billy that she was most surprised and pleased to get—his very own copy of Mother Goose Rhymes.

The next day the Trescowes returned to see Emily. While they signed the adoption papers, Sister Matias helped Emily pack quickly. Sister Agnessa shook Elliot's hand. She gave Norah the yellow blanket that Emily was wrapped in when she was left at the door of the orphanage. As Emily turned to go, she stopped. She ran back to Billy to give him one last hug. "I love you, Billy! Goodbye, goodbye!" Running back to the Trescowes, she let Elliot lift her into the carriage.

Emily waved to her friends as Norah said, "Come on, Emily. Let's get you home."

Jock was at work finalizing the plans for the Calais run. Lace, wool, tobacco and rum were the items they would be taking from France. This was going to be his largest run yet, and he wanted everything to go as smoothly as possible. He decided to charter a 90-ton lugger from the Bodrugan shipyard near Mevagissey. They were known for building luggers with long bowsprits. That, and their sail-area, gave them extra speed.

Jock had already contacted his French cohorts to arrange the time and place for picking up the merchandise. He made sure that they would return to Cornwall during a new moon—the traditional time that smugglers chose to land their crafts on the beach as there was no moonlight to expose their venture. It took several days to get a reply from the French agreeing to his suggested rendezvous plans. He would need to hire more men and ensure that they all carried side-arms. This was never a problem, as Jim Bodrugan always knew which seaworthy men were ready to go at a moment's notice.

Jeremy would be his eyes and ears on land, making sure that the unloading of the contraband would go without a hitch. The townspeople would assist in stowing the cargo in the tunnel that led to the cellars of Tremorna Orphanage. For their efforts they would each receive a small portion of the illegal goods as payment.

Jock had set the date for a week from Sunday. It would take two days to get to Calais, two days to load the goods and have a spot of fun, and two days to get back to Mevagissey. It would take another day to unload the goods into smaller pilchard boats. They would set sail to reach Holly Bay by nightfall. Jock sat back with a satisfied smile on his face. If all went as planned, he would be back in Sal's bed in less than a fortnight.

—o—O—o—

Tommy waited in the dining room for Sister Matias to make her morning rounds. He was anxious. He had never given anyone a gift before. Would she like it? He looked at the piece of wood in his hands. He examined it from all angles to make sure it was good enough. He had to admit that it was the best work he'd ever done.

"Good morning, Tommy. You are up early today. Is this a special occasion?"

Nervous, Tommy all but shoved the whittled boat into her hands. "Here, Sister. I 'ope ye like it."

Sister Matias looked down at the boat. "Oh, Tommy! This is amazing! It truly is!" She admired the intricate carving, especially the designs on each side of the boat. Sister Matias gave Tommy a bear hug. "Thank you, Tommy. I will treasure it always." Tommy stood there, red-faced yet again, as she swept out of the room.

CHAPTER 23

Whistler sat on a stool in the Owler downing his fourth shot of brandy. "Take it easy, mate. One more and ye'll be on the floor!" Jock laughed. Everyone knew that Whistler could not hold his liquor.

"Ach!" Whistler growled. "Leave me be. I'm payin' fer it ain't I? Isshh money in yer pocket. Yer makin' off of yer friends. Sso wha' ye grumblin' 'bout! Sssal! He shouted. "Gi' usss another un."

Sal stood before him, hands on hips. "I think ye've 'ad enough, 'arry. Why don't ye go off 'ome and sleep it off, eh?"

"Ahh ... shite, woman," Whistler mumbled as he stood and fell into Jeremy sitting next to him. Righting himself, he staggered out of the Owler, but not before he swiped a bottle of whiskey.

Whistler was anxious about Calais. He'd never been gone from home that long before, and he had a strong dislike for the French. "Sssome-thin' ssquirmy 'bout 'em. Sslithery like frogs, they isshh. Don't care to 'ave no dealings with 'em. No sssir, I don'. Damn frogs."

Whistler made a quick sign of the cross as he passed the graveyard. He decided he needed a rest and plopped down on the grass, leaning against a tombstone bearing the name "Isaac Trevellyan." He opened the bottle of whiskey and lifted it. " 'Ere'sss to ye, Isssac!" he shouted. He began to sing loudly, "… a good ssword an' a trusty 'and! A merry 'eart an' true! King Jamess'ss men shall unnersstand wha' Cornish ladsss can do!"

Father Cotter was sitting in his study preparing his Sunday sermon. It was a beautiful night, and he had opened the window. Mrs. Martin, his cook and housekeeper, was visiting her son and his wife for the day. He had the rectory to himself. He liked it that way. No Mrs. Martin flitting about straightening and dusting while he tried to concentrate. Suddenly he heard what vaguely resembled singing coming from the churchyard. He put down his quill pen, irritated. "Now who could that be at this hour of the night?"

He stepped out into the warm breeze. The singing grew more raucous. "An' 'ave they fixed the where an' when? An' shall Trelawny die?" It seemed the noise was coming from behind a tombstone near the northeast corner of the graveyard. He made haste to see who it was. All he needed was for the revenue men to come riding by and stop to investigate.

"Out ssspake their capt'n brave an' bold!"

"Shh!"

"Ach! Ye scared the shite out o' me! Thought it were ol' Isaac comin' out o' the groun'!"

"Harry, is that you?" the priest whispered hoarsely. "Get up man! And be quiet or you'll bring Hawker down on us." Father attempted to assist Whistler to his feet but was shoved aside. "Away wi' ye, Father. Leave me be."

"I will Harry, but I want you gone—now!" Father Cotter started toward the rectory door when Whistler, struggling to his feet, shouted, "We be goin' to France, ye know! To the devil'ss land to get us the devil'ss goods!"

Father ran toward Whistler and shook him soundly. "Hold your tongue, man! I'm warning you!"

"Goin' to bring back lotsss of lovliesss for the ladiesss!" Harry trumpeted. The priest shook him again, and Whistler tried to push him away. The smuggler lost his balance and fell, hitting his head sharply against a tombstone.

"Harry! Get up!" The churchyard was now as silent as the souls who lay beneath. Father Cotter bent down and shook Whistler, to no avail. The half-moon shone on dark blood pooled under his head. A minute passed as Father Cotter stared at Whistler's body. He turned away amazed and perplexed. He had never seen a man's neck twisted in such a manner.

Suddenly the realization of what just happened struck Father Cotter. A prickly, cold fear crept up his spine as he sunk to his knees. Looking up, he cried aloud, "Help me, Lord! What have I done?"

"Whoa, whoa there lad!" Roger almost collided with Tommy. "Where are you going? Or should I ask where you've been? It's a little late for you to be out and about. Don't the nuns have a curfew for you to follow?"

"I ... I been down to the beach for a swim," Tommy stammered as he tried to walk away.

"Not so fast, Tommy. I want a word with you." Roger looked Tommy up and down. "So you went down to the beach and then changed your mind? Your clothes are as dry as an old lady's lips."

As Jeremy climbed up the bank from the cove, he overheard the revenue man questioning Tommy. "Leave 'im alone, 'awker!" he shouted. "The lad ain't done nothin' wrong."

"I have every right to question a boy who is out after curfew. Besides, it's none of your business. It's not like he's your son. What are you doing out so late, mister?"

" 'Avin' a swim." Jeremy shook his dripping locks. "Ye should try it—by the smell o' ye!"

Watching Jeremy and Roger spar was almost fun, but Tommy knew this would be the time to take his leave. Tiptoeing backwards until he knew they weren't paying him any mind, he turned and made a dash for the orphanage.

CHAPTER 24

Her mind in a whirl, Sister Therese fell down on her knees and prayed to God to help her keep Jeremy away from Tommy. "It's been a few days now Lord, and he's not come pounding on the door, demanding to see me. Please keep us safe, especially Tommy."

She now realized that Jeremy was indeed the man she saw talking to Tommy after the cricket match. Could he see any resemblance between two-year-old Matthew and fifteen-year-old Tommy? She didn't think so. She closed her eyes and remembered Matthew as a quiet, shy baby. Tommy was almost a man now—and a bit of a wild one at that. No. Thankfully Tommy looked nothing like he did when he was younger. She stayed on her knees praying for guidance. After over an hour of talking to her Lord, she finally felt peaceful. She would be safe if she ceased any outings and stayed within the confines of the orphanage. She was going to go to the Reverend Mother first thing in the morning and tell her everything. She hoped she would, or could, be forgiven. Whatever happened after that was in God's hands.

Sister Therese wasn't the only one on her knees that night. Father Cotter had prayed and prayed, yet God did not answer. Remorse hung heavy as he pleaded for forgiveness, but none came. He laid wide awake atop his bed. He couldn't get the horrific picture of Whistler's twisted neck out of his head. In a panic, he had dragged Whistler to a newly dug grave. Maggie Tippet, a tight-lipped spinster, was to be buried the next morning. The priest unceremoniously rolled Whistler into the open grave and winced at the thud. He covered him with dirt. Strangely, it was not lost on the priest that poor teetotaling Maggie would have to spend eternity lying atop drunken Harry Drake.

Maggie Tippet was buried without incident or mourners. Father Cotter breathed a sigh of relief as the last mound of dirt was shoveled over her. That night, however, he heard noises in the churchyard. Was that Hawker and his men? Would they never stop hounding him? Now the noises sounded like loud footsteps. The crunching of shovels digging followed, even louder. Father Cotter put his hands to his ears to block out the sounds. His heart was pounding. Suddenly someone tapped him on the shoulder. "I didn't do it! I didn't do it!" he cried. He felt like his heart would burst.

"Are you alright, Father?"

Exhaling shakily, he looked up. It was Mrs. Martin, bless her heart! He managed a nod. She stared at him oddly then quickly turned away.

The next morning, Father Cotter looked out the window of his study. He could see Maggie's grave from there. He was shocked to see that nothing had been disturbed. The dirt had not been touched.

It had been two days before anyone realized that Whistler was missing. No one had seen him at the Owler, which was very unusual. He practically lived there. Jock called his men together, and they began to search for him. He knew that Whistler was not overly excited about the Calais run. Maybe he was laying low, hoping they would leave without him. Whatever the reason, Jock would feel better if he found him before they left for France.

Two of Jock's men were making their way through the churchyard. When they passed Maggie Tippet's grave they paused. Looking down, both made the sign of the cross. They walked toward the rectory and rapped on the door.

Mrs. Martin opened the door and was surprised to see them standing there. "Yes?"

One of the men tipped his dirt-encrusted cap. "Mornin', miz. Is the pastor at 'ome?"

Mrs. Martin, suspicious by nature, looked the men up and down. "Wha' ye want 'im fer?"

"We be lookin' fer Whistler. Been searchin' the village. Thought Father Cotter might know somethin'."

"Well, 'e's 'ere, but 'e ain't to be bothered. " 'Sides, 'e's been in 'is study all day."

"Whistler went missin' a few days ago. Just want to know when the priest saw 'im last."

"Who wants to know?"

"Jock Hastings, miz, landlord an' owner o' the Owler."

Mrs. Martin knew Jock. She'd spent a shilling or two in his establishment. She and Jock's wife Sal had become fast friends over the years.

"I'll ask 'im when I brings 'is supper to 'im. I'll get word to Jock."

Both men tipped their caps to her. "Thank ye kindly, miz."

When Mrs. Martin shut the door, she noticed that the study door was open a crack. She peeked inside. There was no sign of Father Cotter.

When Sister Therese woke up that morning, doubts had already crept in. Would she be doing the right thing by telling the Reverend Mother about her past? Would she be asked to leave the only safe place she'd ever known? Would Tommy have to leave too? Kerena looked up. "Lord, please go before me and prepare the way. I know whatever happens, you will be with me. Amen."

As Kerena knocked on Sister Agnessa's door, she closed her eyes and whispered, "Give me strength, Lord."

"Come in."

Kerena took a deep breath and entered.

Father Cotter had overheard the conversation between Mrs. Martin and Jock's men. He made haste to leave the rectory out the back door and hurried to the church. He ran to the front near the altar and fell on his knees begging for forgiveness. He broke down weeping when suddenly he heard a shuffling noise at the back of the church. His hair stood on end. He closed his eyes and turned slowly in the direction of the sound. When he opened his eyes there was nothing there—only silence. He fell back onto the front pew, shaking with relief. Sobbing inconsolably, he laid down on the hard pew and eventually fell asleep.

When he awoke, Father Cotter sat up and realized it was late. He'd missed his supper. He trudged to the back of the church and through the doorway that led to the churchyard. "Trelawny 'e's in keep in hold: Trelawny he may die ..."

The priest stopped. He recognized the words of the old Cornish folk song. "Who's that singing?" he demanded. He swung around, tripping on his robes and fell at the foot of Maggie Tippet's grave. "But here's twenty thousand Cornish bold will know the reason why!"

"No! No! No!" he cried as he righted himself and ran full-tilt back to the rectory.

Sister Agnessa sat back in her chair astounded by the startling confession of Kerena Dugan. She knew she would need to handle this situation with care, for it seemed that Kerena was beginning to unravel. "Sister Therese—Kerena—perhaps you'd like to go to your room and rest. It took a lot for you to tell me your story, and I am grateful that you did. It is quite a lot to take in, and I'd like some time to think and pray. You understand, I am sure." Kerena nodded. She was exhausted and numbed after her confession.

"I want you to know that no matter what happens, no matter what decisions are made, Tommy— Matthew—is our main concern. I do have one more question, Kerena. Does Tommy know you are his mother?"

"No, Sister. He hasn't seen me since he was two years old. When I first came to this orphanage, I didn't know he had been sent here. I guessed who he was from records showing that a little boy named Tommy had arrived here. You already know that I had changed my boy's name from Matthew to Tommy." Kerena paused, then looked down trying to still her shaking hands. "I have tried to stay in the background whenever he is near. The few times he did see me, he showed no sign of knowing who I was."

The Reverend Mother nodded. "It may be the habit that is hiding your identity from him. I think it best we keep him in the dark for as long as possible, for his safety."

Kerena looked up at the Reverend Mother, gratitude filling her heart. "Thank you, Reverend Mother. That is all I ask and all I've prayed for."

When Kerena left the room, Sister Agnessa leaned forward, her mind spinning with countless thoughts. In all her years as a nun, she had never heard a story quite like this. She was humbled by the courage of this poor girl. She didn't know if she would have done the same thing if she were in such a situation. With Kerena's husband out of prison and possibly in the vicinity, Sister Agnessa knew that the most important thing right now was to ensure the safety of Matthew Dugan. He had to be protected at all costs.

CHAPTER 25

The search continued for Whistler. The last time anyone saw him was when he left the Owler three nights ago very tipsy and singing loudly off-key. All very normal. No one ever gave it a second thought. Whistler lived just a few cottages down from the Owler and had always made it home. He was usually the last one to leave the pub as he had no one to go home to and detested living alone. "The Owler's me real 'ome," he was heard to say many times.

The atmosphere in the pub became rather subdued. It wasn't the same without old Whistler to liven things up. Jock and Sal were really getting worried. Jock even made a visit to Roger Hawker to see if he had seen or heard of Whistler's whereabouts. Harry was nowhere to be found.

Jock met with his crew. "Much as I 'ate leaving for Calais wi'out Whistler, we need to stick to our plan. We leave tomorrow night. We meet at Port Pentruth at midnight. We'll sail for Mevagissey where we'll dock our boats. There'll be more men waiting for us aboard the lugger we're takin' to France."

"Sure won't be the same wi'out Whistler and Lundy," some of the men murmured as they left for home to pack their gear.

The next morning Father Cotter awoke in a fog. He had tapped into the Communion wine the night before after the horrific incident near Maggie's grave. "Am I losing my mind?" he thought. "Did I imagine someone singing?" He tried to clear his head. He had a class to teach today at the orphanage, and he hadn't even prepared for it. Maybe he'd just ask the children what Bible story they'd like to hear.

As he left the rectory, he took a different path to avoid the churchyard. Halfway to the orphanage, he heard a voice whisper, "Sssso cold …"

"Whistler? Is that you?" The priest spun around, fear etched in his face like frost. "What am I saying? It's can't be Whistler can it? But it sounded like Whistler." Father Cotter had heard of hauntings but had never believed in them. His father had always said it was nothing but gibberish.

When he arrived at the classroom, he was visibly shaken. The children wondered if something was wrong but were afraid to ask. "G-good morning, children. Today I am going to let one of you decide which Bible story you would like to hear." He looked around the room as many hands went up. "Pudgie, what would you like me to read for this morning's lesson?"

"Lazarus! Let's 'ear 'bout Lazarus!" Pudgie yelled. The rest of the class shouted enthusiastically, "Yes! Give us Lazarus!"

"I like the part where Lazarus comes back from the dead. I wonder what 'e looked like. Pretty spooky, I'm thinkin'," another student surmised.

"Probably 'is face was sunk in by then, don't ye think? An' maybe 'is eyes stuck out too," yet another student elaborated.

"And 'is teeth! Maybe 'e 'ad a grinnin' skull!" someone shouted excitedly. Father Cotter's face grew greyer with each remark.

"That's enough, children," Sister Agnessa admonished. She had been watching Father Cotter. He didn't look at all well. She went to the front of the classroom and whispered to the priest, "Are you alright, Father? Would you like to sit down? Could I get you some water?"

As Father Cotter looked up, the room began to spin. He took a firm hold of Sister Agnessa's hand and whispered, "I think I need to lie down, Sister."

"Yes, Father, right away." The Reverend Mother motioned for Pudgie to come to the front of the classroom. "Pudgie, I want you to begin reading the story of Lazarus to the rest of the class. Father Cotter is not feeling well, and I am taking him to see Sister Hildegard. I will be right back."

As the Sister and the priest left the room, Pudgie stood there for a moment. He had never been asked to read from the Bible before. He liked the idea of running the class though, even if it was for just a few minutes. He puffed out his chest and said, "Class, please listen as I read the passage and be ready with questions afterwards." Liza threw a piece of chalk at Pudgie's head, and the rest of the class burst into laughter.

As Sister Agnessa was returning to the classroom, it struck her that Father Cotter had smelled strongly of wine. "Now what could that be all about?" she wondered.

Jock had sailed to Mevagissey a few times and never got tired of seeing the pretty little fishing village. The cottages were crowded together on lanes so narrow, only very small carts were able to pass each other. The harbor was packed with boats, most of which were sailing vessels. Their masts stood up like a forest of naked trees. Men in rugged boots and shabby guernseys were loading and unloading goods.

Jock and his men sailed from Mevagissey on the Godolphin. It was not the largest lugger by far but sufficient for the needs of his 30-man crew and its business. That evening they sat around the galley fire devouring pasties and downing mugs of grog to keep warm. Exciting tales were told by each man in his turn: brave buccaneers, royalist scoundrels, and bawdy wenches—all seemed to figure in every telling. Most stories had some version of a musket ball finding someone's eye. Songs of the sea were sung, words barely remembered, until they retired, each to their berth. They were lulled to sleep by the rise and fall of the waves and the rigging creaking above their heads.

Near dusk the next day, as they came into the Strait of Dover, one of the crew pointed out the well-known white cliffs of Dover. They were now at the narrowest point of the English Channel. Soon they would see the belfry of the town hall of Calais. The watchtower Tour de Guet acted as a lighthouse, guiding the ships in and out of the harbor. The crew slept aboard the Godolphin that night, but not before slaking their thirst at the Porte a la Mer Inn. Upon entering, they noticed paintings of dames de la nuit in tantalizing positions, hanging crookedly along one wall. A card game was heating up at one table—drunken Frenchies shouting angry remarks at each other.

Jock walked to the bar, sat on a rusty metal stool, and ordered a whiskey. Although his men would likely get drunk, he was meeting with his French counterparts in the morning and needed to keep his head. Jock had always felt uncomfortable in his dealings with the French. He didn't trust them. They were conniving thieves who wouldn't think twice about slitting your throat to earn a few sou. He'd be glad to see the back of them.

Summoned to the Reverend Mother's office, Kerena's heart was in her throat. She had not spoken to Sister Agnessa since she had confessed everything to her. She knew her fate and that of her son was in the Reverend Mother's hands. Knowing that this may be the most important meeting of her life, she hesitated, then rapped on the door and entered.

"Good morning, Sister Therese. Please sit down." Sister Agnessa looked solemn. "I have been praying about your situation and have made some decisions." She looked directly at Kerena. Kerena gulped audibly. "This needs to be kept between ourselves, Sister. No one else can be told. It would only jeopardize your safety as well as Tommy's. A council of bishops will be gathering in London in a few months' time. They will make the final decision as to whether you will be allowed to continue in your role as a nun. As you have studied and taken your vows in good faith, I see no reason for you to leave us at this time. You may in the future feel that that is what you need to do. For now, you are welcome to stay. Tommy also."

Relief flooded Kerena. It appeared that her past had not yet caught up to her. She thanked the Reverend Mother for her forgiveness and understanding. As they both stood, Sister Agnessa said, "You say that you may have seen your husband in the area. Be very careful, Kerena. Do not leave the premises under any circumstances. It's too great a risk."

"I won't, Sister."

CHAPTER 26

Mary had offered to walk a very shaky Father Cotter back to the rectory on her way home. Sister Hildegard had checked him over and found him in good health physically. "No need for a doctor," she said to Mary. "A good night of sleep and some hot tea will do him a world of good."

The priest was quiet as they strolled together along the cliff path. Mary was worried. He didn't seem as well as Sister Hildegard suggested. Even in the growing darkness she could see he was deathly pale. He stumbled so often that Mary had to hang on to him tightly. She was having a difficult time keeping him upright.

As they reached the churchyard, Mary offered to walk him to the rectory door, but he stopped her and said, "Thank you, Mary. That's not necessary. I'll be fine. Mrs. Martin will most likely be in a tither about where I've been. Th-thank you again. You are most kind," he mumbled as he began to make his way, unsteadily, through the tombstones.

Father Cotter was near the rectory when he passed the grave of Isaac Trevellyn. He looked down and saw a dark area on the bottom corner of the headstone. As he recalled the events that led to Whistler's death, he noticed the bloodstain growing larger. Panic overtook him.

He let out a shrill scream and didn't stop until a distraught Mrs. Martin came running. She was able to calm him down enough to get him inside the rectory. As she closed the door, he slumped to the floor mumbling incoherently. She fixed some chamomile tea for him and added the herb St. John's Wort. This should have eased his anxiety, but it didn't. He babbled something about "Isaac" and would periodically call out Whistler's name. Hearing his disjointed words only confused her more.

Mrs. Martin stayed with him the rest of the night while he dozed fitfully. He would awaken agitated and continue to call out to Whistler. "F-forgive me, Whistler!"

"Whistler forgive Father Cotter?" Mrs. Martin wondered. "But why?"

The housekeeper grew even more perplexed when, as dawn broke, Father Cotter had not come out of his delirium. She kept him as quiet as possible, knowing that she needed to get the doctor. Thankfully, about an hour later, there was a knock on the rectory door. It was Mary coming to check on him. "How is he this morning, Mrs. Martin? Did he sleep well?"

"Oh, our Mary! I be that fearful! I need to get the doc right away! I think 'e's got a fever o' the brain!"

At that moment, Father Cotter awoke and shouted "F-forgive me!" Mary ran into his room. His bedclothes were curled up in a ball on the floor, and the teacup that his housekeeper had left on the nightstand lay in shards on the floor. Mary quickly covered him with a quilt. As she did so, he grabbed her hand and spoke the first sane words he'd spoken since he got home. "Get Roger, Mary. Get him now!"

Jeremy sat at a table in the Owler planning his strategy for landing the goods coming in from France. He needed to ensure there was enough manpower to unload and then spirit the contraband quickly into hiding. Although his mind was on his work, thoughts of Kerena and Matthew crept in. When he ran into Roger Hawker and Tommy the other night, he had felt a strange connection with the lad. He remembered what Hawker had said. "It's not like he's your son."

"I hope Matthew grew up to be like Tommy. 'E's got pluck," Jeremy thought. Matthew would be about the same age as Tommy.

Suddenly, Jeremy remembered the nun he had run into in the village. Something in the tone of the nun's voice reminded him of Kerena, and the way she ran off so quick-like, he reflected. Could it be? Could Kerena have become a nun? But how could she? She's married!

Then it all started to fall into place. Kerena never wanted Matthew to follow in his footsteps. Hadn't he threatened to come back and take Matthew from her? If Kerena did become a nun to hide from him, surely Matthew would be with her. He just had to find out where!

—o—O—o—

Roger was sitting across from Father Cotter in the rectory kitchen. Mrs. Martin had just served tea. When she left the room, Roger spoke first. "Now, Father, tell me what this is all about. Mary was quite frantic when she came to me this morning. I got here as fast as I could." Roger could plainly see that the priest was quite distraught. He waited patiently.

"Mr. Hawker. I-I need to tell you about what I've done. I have to tell someone. I can't live like this anymore. The haunting has got to stop!"

Roger was surprised to hear this coming from a priest but remained calm. "Haunting, Father?"

"Y-yes! It seems everywhere I go he's there! The singing! The blood! He won't leave me alone!"

Roger narrowed his eyes. "What is it you think you've done, Father?"

Father Cotter started to sob. "I killed him! I killed poor Whistler! I didn't mean to, but I did!"

Roger inhaled sharply. In fits and starts, the priest explained how it happened. Roger could see that Whistler's death was an accident. It was what Father Cotter did with Whistler's body that astounded the revenue man. How a man could even think about doing something so awful was hard enough to swallow—but a priest?

Roger had heard enough, but it seemed that Father Cotter wasn't finished with his confession. He told Roger all he knew of Jock's smuggling trip to Calais and when he was expected to return. He told him of the tunnel leading to the orphanage cellars. He even told him of the signal given from the orphanage window. Roger was mystified! Were these statements true or just the ravings of a lunatic? Regardless, Roger knew what he must do. He knew that Mary was waiting outside with a cart. From what Mary had told him earlier, he wanted to be ready in case they needed to transport the priest to a hospital.

"I'm sorry, Father, but I have to take you in. I'll need you to repeat your story to others and give us your oath that it's true. We will have questions and will need to know more about Jock and his men and their plans. I will tell Mrs. Martin not to expect you back for at least a few days."

Father Cotter sighed, then nodded his head. He got to his feet, immediately losing his balance. "Mary! Come quickly! Help me!"

Roger shouted. After getting Father Cotter settled in the back of the cart, Mary and Roger slowly drove the cart away. Father Cotter sat forlornly against the wooden-slatted side, chewing on his lips nervously. He looked like a small, cornered animal. Mrs. Martin stood in the doorway, her apron held up to her eyes. The cart rattled through the churchyard and out through the gate.

That morning, Jeremy was walking into town when he saw Mr. Terwilliger's wagon clanking down the lane. "Mornin' sir. 'Aven't seen ye around 'ere afore. Is there anythin' ye need?"

"Mornin' tinker. Don' need nothin' 'cept information."

"Oh, I got lots o' that to go 'round. What is it yer after?"

"Are there any convents nearby?"

"Convents, ye say? Well, now, let me see. ... Closest one I know is near Bude. That's a ways away. Might ye be needin' a ride?"

"I just might at that. Are ye goin' that way?"

"Just came from 'round there. Be goin' back in a day or so. I'll be on this same road if ye're interested."

Jeremy tipped his hat to Mr. Terwilliger. He continued his walk into town when the tinker stopped his cart. "Say, mister! There do be nuns live at the orphanage 'ere."

Jeremy thanked the man and smiled devilishly as he changed direction. Now he was heading toward Tremorna Orphanage.

Tommy was getting excited about Jock's return. He ran up to the top floor of the orphanage to check that everything was ready to send the signal. Then he ran back down to the dining room for breakfast, running right into Sister Therese. "Whoa there, Tommy. Slow down. Are you that hungry for Cook's pancakes?"

"You bet I am, Sister! 'Specially when there's blueberries in 'em!" he shouted as he scooted past her, taking his seat at the table. In spite of Kerena's worries about Jeremy, she had to laugh at Tommy's antics. He seemed so happy. She didn't want anything to happen to change that.

Meanwhile, Jeremy had been lurking about the gardens of the orphanage just waiting for a glimpse of whom he hoped was Kerena. Luck was on his side. He saw a nun step out of the side door. She stayed close to the door, never moving away from it. She looked up, as if breathing in the fresh air. Jeremy saw her face and knew it was Kerena. He made his move.

After further questioning of Father Cotter, it was clear to Roger that the man was in a bad way. He would not be able to return to his duties for a long time to come—maybe never. Roger had sent an inquiry by horseback messenger to the St. Lawrence Lunatic Asylum, a fairly new institution in Bodmin. He hoped they would accept Father Cotter as a patient. In the meantime, Father Cotter was held in a small cell in Tremorna. They kept prisoners there until they were dispatched either to Bodmin Jail or Newgate Prison in London or assigned to a work crew in

Australia. As sad as the situation was, Roger had more important things to think about. Time was running out.

CHAPTER 27

Jock's crew was heading home, loaded with cargo. They had strung over 100 kegs of spirits from bow to stern on both sides of the vessel. Once the kegs were cut loose, Jeremy and his land crew would help float the goods ashore. Jock was satisfied with the transactions they had made in Calais. He stood near the bow of the ship. "It will be good to get back 'ome though," he thought. "A pint o' frothy ale and a couple o' Scotch eggs is what I need. No more o' that Frenchie food fer me!" Some of his men began singing, their voices getting louder as they reached the coast of Cornwall. Tired and smelly, they stood behind Jock, watching excitedly as the port of Mevagissey came into view.

Jeremy grabbed Kerena by the arm and didn't let go. She looked Jeremy in the eye and spat. As spittle oozed down his face, Jeremy grabbed her by the other arm and shook her soundly. "So, ye're a nun now, eh? Is that wha' they teach ye in nun school—how to spit in yer 'usband's eye? But nuns don' 'ave 'usbands, do they, Sister Kerena? Or wha'ever ye call yerself now."

Kerena looked at him with pure hatred. She knew she was caught. There was no way to squirm out of this mess she'd gotten herself into. "I didn't think ye were ever comin' back. I 'ad to find a way to support Matthew and meself. And it's Sister Therese now. Kerena no longer exists, at least in the eyes o' the church."

"The eyes o' the church!" Jeremy hissed. "The eyes o' the church 'ad better look a little closer then! My God, Kerena! Ye're a married woman with a son—my son!" Jeremy pushed Kerena away in disgust. He knew she wasn't going anywhere. "Matthew's 'ere then, isn't 'e! I want to see 'im. NOW!"

Kerena jumped back. She had to tell him, but the words wouldn't come.

Jeremy glared at her. Then his countenance changed, as if something just dawned on him. He paused. Then he spoke deliberately and menacingly. "It's Tommy. Ye changed Matthew's name to 'ide 'im from me. Aye, that's it. I knew when I saw Tommy there was somethin' about 'im. I'm right, ain't I!"

Kerena could only nod. Suddenly a wave of weariness and, strangely, relief swept over her. She fainted at his feet.

Roger finally received word that the asylum in Bodmin would accept the priest as a patient. Roger and Mary helped Mrs. Martin pack Father Cotter's personal belongings, and he was taken to Bodmin by two of Roger's revenue men. It was a sad picture watching Father Cotter being led away. No one gave a thought to how the church would carry on.

Roger gathered the rest of his men and planned for the return of Jock and his crew. They knew the time he was expected to land in Holly

Bay. They knew someone would signal them to come ashore. They just had to lay in wait and seize the crew and the stolen goods when they landed. Roger would send some of his men out in small boats to surround the bay. Those men would watch and wait for as long as it took. The rest of his men would be waiting on shore.

Roger still couldn't believe his luck. Father Cotter was a bit shaken and confused when he confessed what he knew about the Calais run. However, he did seem to know specific details about the day and time of the return of Jock's crew and what they would be carrying onboard. This was Roger's best chance yet of nabbing this smuggling ring once and for all. "They've always been a thorn in my side—the crew that can't be captured! Well, this time I'll get 'em!" he crowed.

Tommy found Kerena laying just outside the orphanage door. "Sister Therese! Wake up!" he shouted, shaking her until her eyes sprung open.

"Wha' happened?" Kerena mumbled, still in a daze. Tommy helped her to sit up, and as she became more aware, fear and panic began to surface. "Tommy! Y-your father…"

Before Kerena could say more, Sister Hildegard and the Reverend Mother came rushing out the door and assisted Kerena to her feet. They led her into the kitchen as Tommy hollered, "Wait! Do ye know somethin' 'bout me da?"

"Shh, Tommy. Not now," The Reverend Mother scolded. "Sister Therese is in no shape to answer any of your questions. Go and help Cook and Winnie with the breakfast dishes if you've nothing better to do."

As they walked Sister Therese to the infirmary, Tommy stood there puzzled. What could Sister Therese know about his father? Did she know him? Did she know his mother too? Tommy absentmindedly began wiping a stack of washed plates. He had to talk to her soon!

That evening, Tommy was down on the beach watching for anything unusual. On a moonless night you had to be extra careful! He turned to run up the steps to the orphanage. Soon he would send the signal that it was safe for Jock and his men to come ashore. Then he saw something on the beach. It looked like a revenue man getting into a boat further down the cove. Using the spyglass that Jock had given him, he looked out over the water as far as he could see. It was very dark, but his eyes were now accustomed to it. By straining, he could see that boats were dotting the entire area surrounding Holly Bay. Revenue vessels, they were. He was sure of it!

Glad he hadn't given the signal yet, Tommy turned to see that the lamp in the window had indeed been lit. He was shocked and bewildered! Staring at the window, he saw a shadow back out of sight. Who was it? He quickly realized it didn't matter who it was—the deed was done! Wasting no time, Tommy ran to the tunnels where a spare rowboat was stored. He had to warn Jock somehow. As he pulled the boat toward the tide, a shot rang out, and Tommy fell to the ground.

Jeremy heard the shot and saw Tommy drop. "No!" he screamed, as he ran toward his son. He was immediately grabbed from behind by two of Roger's men. While he struggled to loosen their hold, he screamed, "Tommy! Matthew!" He saw Tommy's head lift up from the sand briefly. Kicking wildly at his captors, Jeremy managed to connect with one man's shin while clawing at the face of the other. Freeing himself, he ran blindly, stumbling in the sand to reach his son. Before the men caught up to him he managed to cry out, "Don' ruin yer life like I did, Son! See what 'appens?" Tommy barely heard Jeremy's words before passing out.

Jeremy turned just as a revenue man brought the stock of his gun down on him. It slammed into his face, breaking his nose and knocking him out. Blood spurted out from his face as he lay on the beach. He was dragged away to the booming sounds of muskets and flintlock pistols firing from all directions.

Jock and his crew were struggling to keep their boats steady in all of the confusion. They were not only being fired upon from the shore but from the revenue men's boats as well. The smugglers tried to row away while ducking down. They couldn't tell if the musket balls were high or low. They knew some were close because they could hear ptew when they struck the water. Few hit their targets, but they were large and deadly projectiles. Jock stood in his boat to fire blindly when he was hit in the leg. His right thigh bone shattered. He screamed in pain and fell overboard. His rowers kept rowing away from him in their haste to get away. When he surfaced, he looked straight into the eyes of two revenue men. Unable to swim away, he was seized and pulled roughly into their vessel while he gasped for breath and bled uncontrollably.

A woman was bludgeoned while wading out to find her husband. One smuggler almost made it to shore but died at the edge of the water, a large, bloody hole where his stomach used to be. Another was dropped just yards away, a hot musket ball buried in the back of his head. On the beach, a furious, frustrated revenue man confronted a slight, toothless old fisherman who served as a cook aboard one of the luggers. The pathetic little criminal begged for mercy, but the built-up hatred of the king's man would not be denied. He shoved his bayonet up into the man's chest and ripped it out of his throat. The revenue man grinned as the cook, wide-eyed and gurgling, collapsed on the sand.

The sickening melee finally came to an end. Both sides suffered losses during the nightmarish raid. Most were Jock's men, who were unprepared for a full-scale battle. They were surprised by the welcoming parties both on land and sea. Some of the smugglers were able to escape, most within an inch of their lives. Those who were captured watched as their boats, loaded with contraband, were confiscated by Roger Hawker's men. They knew their freedom and futures were also taken.

Townspeople gathered on the beach, awed by the sight, as torn and fish-eyed bodies bobbed and floated to shore. Their blood turned the waves a deep, dark red. Men bowed and shook their heads. Women wailed. A stray child sobbed her tears onto her father's broken body. She begged him to "please come 'ome," while looking into open eyes that would never see her again. More blood was shed that night than any other in the history of Holly Bay.

CHAPTER 28

The children were awakened by the sounds of shots being fired. Pudgie's room looked out over the bay. He ran to his window and saw several bright flashes followed by the loud booms of gunfire. Torches and lanterns lit up the gruesome scene being played out below.

Billy ran down the stairs shouting, "We heard shots! We heard shots! And Tommy's not in 'is room!" Sister Matias came out of her room and ran to Billy. He backed away for a second. He'd never seen Sister Matias without her habit and wimple. She was wearing only a flowing white gown, her shorn hair matted. She had not heard a thing. Her room was on the opposite side of the building. She was sleeping like a baby when she heard Billy's cries.

Suddenly, Billy pointed to the front door of the orphanage. It was wide open. Puzzled, they went to wake the Reverend Mother. By this time, Sister Hildegard and Tessa the cook were awake and came running into the foyer. "Where is Sister Therese?" the Reverend Mother asked. No one knew. Sister Matias ran to the nun's room, but she wasn't there. Sister Agnessa thought for a moment. "I have an idea where she might have gone. Come with me, Sister Hildegard. Sister Matias, please stay with the children, and calm them if you can."

Sister Therese, always a light sleeper, had heard the first musket fire. She rushed to Tommy's room, finding his bed empty. "Oh no," she groaned. Giving no thought to her appearance, she flew out the front door and down to the cove as fast as she could. The scene before her was devastating. Cudgels were swung. Bodies were dropped. Townspeople tripped over mangled limbs as they ran for safety. Suddenly she heard Jeremy yelling Tommy's name. She ran in the direction of his voice. There lay Tommy, blood pouring from his side. She ran to him, screaming his name over and over. Falling to her knees, she lifted Tommy's head onto her lap. One of the townspeople heard her cries and ran to her. "Please, help me get him to the orphanage! Quick!" By this time Sister Agnessa and Sister Hildegard arrived at Tommy's side, looking like twin ghosts, their nightgowns slowly billowing out around them in the near dark. They lifted Tommy and carried him to the infirmary. Sister Hildegard tore Tommy's trousers away from his wound, which was still bleeding profusely. It seemed to her that the musket ball had entered his side, ripping a gaping hole as it exited his back. There was no telling if any of his insides had been damaged without a doctor's examination.

After seeing the wounds, the Reverend Mother lost no time in sending Billy and Pudgie to get the wagon ready. "Billy, put a couple of quilts in the back. Pudgie, bring as many clean rags as you can find. We'll need to push down where Tommy's bleeding to hold the blood in until we get to Truro. Hurry!"

— ◦ O ◦ —

Roger Hawker had men stationed on the roads leading in and out of Tremorna. No one was to leave until he had questioned everyone on the beach. When Daniel drove the wagon carrying Tommy to the edge of town, they were stopped. "Sorry, Sister. I can't let ye go. I got me orders."

Sister Therese jumped down from the back of the wagon. "This boy will die without help. Please don't make us disobey you."

The revenue man stepped back, weak-kneed at the sight of her blood-soaked gown. Barely able to speak as he gagged uncontrollably, he squeaked out, "Go, Sister ... ye 'ave me blessin'. I'll say a prayer for the boy." Kerena hopped into the wagon and signaled Daniel to proceed.

Upon arriving at the hospital in Truro, a doctor examined Tommy right away. He assured the sisters that the musket ball had indeed entered and exited Tommy and that nothing inside had been damaged. "The wounds, however, are very large, and he's lost a lot of blood. He has not come around, so he won't feel any pain while we clean him up as best we can. He'll have to stay here for at least a few days. We need to watch for morbid decay." He looked at the bedraggled nuns with compassion. "I suggest you go home. There is nothing you can do for him right now. He needs rest, and so do you. Come back in a few days. Hopefully by then we should know if he'll survive."

"If ye don' mind, Doctor, I'll be stayin'," Sister Therese said. The doctor nodded and told one of the hospital nuns to bring a cot into Tommy's room. He said goodbye to the Reverend Mother and Sister Hildegard. They quietly departed. On the way home, Sister Hildegard asked the Reverend Mother why Sister Therese felt she had to stay. Sister Agnessa gave her a silent look followed by, "Don't ask me why. Just pray for her."

After cleaning the wounds as best he could, the doctor bandaged Tommy's side. All he could do now was hope that no putrefaction would develop. Tommy was insensible but showed no signs of distress, so the doctor left him with a hospital nun and Sister Therese. He said he would be back in the morning.

By the next day Tommy's condition was worse. He thrashed about unaware of all. Kerena was beside herself. When the doctor came, she looked at him and pleaded, "Isn't there anything else you can do, Doctor?"

The boy was clearly feverish. He was sweating profusely, and his breathing was shallow. The doctor looked at Kerena and said, "He's in God's hands now, Sister." He told the hospital nun to try to spoon some tea into him and keep him warm. "Perhaps the fever will break soon," he said and shrugged. As he left the room, he heard Kerena's cries for God's mercy!

A few hours later, a hospital nun brought a tray with a bowl of soup and some tea for Kerena. "Ye must be starved, Sister." Kerena didn't answer. She was at Tommy's side trying to calm him as he tossed about on his cot, nearly tipping it over. He would mumble now and then, but nothing she could understand.

As Kerena wiped the sweat from Tommy's face, he opened his eyes and spoke the first words that she could understand: "Me da—where? …" As the pain gripped him, he succumbed again.

The fever seemed to be getting worse. He was restless but seemed weaker. When Tommy could sleep, Kerena prayed. Exhausted, she finally fell asleep. She awoke to see Tommy had not improved. A hospital nun came into the room. "Sister, there is a woman 'ere to see ye. Shall I send 'er in?" Kerena nodded, wondering who it could be.

When the woman walked in, Kerena remembered her—the gypsy woman Mr. Terwilliger had brought to the orphanage when little Janie Tabbert was so ill. "Maleva?"

"Aye, ye remembered," Maleva smiled as she took Kerena's hand in hers. "I come to 'elp the boy. The ol' tinker 'eard 'bout Tommy and came to get me."

"Oh, I'm so grateful! The doctor says there is nothing more he can do."

"Oh aye, probably not. Most healin' men don' believe in the power of herbs, but plants can be a wonderful 'elp." As Maleva began to prepare a poultice of horsetail herb, she related the story of the elder tree, which is said to be enchanted. "A true portal to the faerie realm—a very sacred and magical plant." When the hospital nun returned, Maleva handed her some elderflower, told her to make a strong tea, and bring it to her.

"I best be doin' this quick-like, as the doc won' 'preciate me doin' 'is job fer 'im," she cackled, her jowls wagging back and forth. She removed the dressings and shook her head. "Don' like the smell o' it." She gently cleansed the gaping wounds and poured honey directly on each. She then wrapped them in seaweed and applied clean dressings. By the time she was finished, the nurse had returned with the tea. The nurse helped hold Tommy's head up while Maleva spoon-fed the warm tea into him. Maleva smiled as Tommy seemed to be taking the tea without coughing it up.

Looking at Kerena, Maleva whispered, " 'E's sleepin' soundly and 'is breathin' is stronger. I'll be back come mornin' to check on the lad. Get some sleep. Let the herbs an' faeries do their work." And with that, she was gone.

It was a somber mood that fell over the townspeople as they stood on the beach the next morning. They couldn't stop staring at the carnage last night's raid left behind. Sal opened the Owler early that day.

Her heart was not in it, but she knew people would need a place to congregate. She was not ignorant of the possible sentence that would be set upon Jock. Not knowing the circumstances of Jock's arrest, she knew that if he had injured or shot at a revenue officer, he could be hung. If he was accused of smuggling goods (which was highly likely), he would at best get seven years in Newgate Prison. Of more concern to Sal, however, were Jock's wounds. She had heard that he had been hit in the leg with a musket ball. If he didn't die from it, he would most certainly lose his leg.

She also thought about poor Tommy. If he got caught, he could get a month of hard labor for signaling the smugglers. Hard labor was not easy for a boy his age. The townspeople had not been able to salvage any of the contraband. This time, that was a lucky break. The sentence for receiving smuggled goods could be three months in prison.

As Sal mulled over the possible fate of the smugglers, Mr. Terwilliger stopped in for his regular pint. He told Sal that Tommy was in hospital and "in a bad way." Sal swayed at the news of his wounds. She was relieved when he told her that Maleva went to see what she could do for Tommy. "If anyone can 'elp the poor boy, it would be Maleva with 'er gypsy potions."

"I'm 'fraid I got more bad news, Mrs. 'astings." Mr. Terwilliger related the story of Father Cotter's confession and how it brought Roger's men their successful outcome of last night's raid. "The poor priest's wits be gone. 'Is brain be addled so bad 'e be sent to the asylum!" Mr. Terwilliger shook his head as he downed his ale. "Don' know wha's to become of 'im."

Sal grabbed a stool and plopped down on it, shocked by this news. "Father Cotter? Who would 'ave ever thought?"

Mr. Terwilliger took Sal's hand. "I got worse news. Father Cotter killed poor ol' Whistler! Claims 'e pushed Whistler onto a gravestone. Says 'e didn't mean to. The priest buried 'im under Maggie Tippet, of all places!"

When Mr. Terwilliger left, Sal closed the Owler for the rest of the day. She sat alone, mourning the loss of Whistler. She wept for the fate of Jock and his men and for the townspeople who were lamenting the loss of loved ones. She hadn't lived through a worse day in her life. She cried until she ran dry, then fell asleep, spent.

Winnie couldn't sleep that night worrying about Tommy. She knew that he had been involved in signaling the smugglers for quite some time. She had warned him of the consequences should he get caught, but she never thought he'd be shot. Tears flowed as she wiped the last supper dish. Tommy and Winnie had become close friends over the years. She would miss him dearly if he didn't pull through.

The Reverend Mother had gathered the nuns and all the children together in the dining room that evening. A rosary was said for Tommy. Sister Agnessa was the only one who knew Sister Therese's shocking secret. She prayed that Kerena would find strength in the Lord to get through this, come what may.

CHAPTER 29

Maleva walked into Tommy's hospital room early the next morning. There was Sister Therese, fast sleep, her cot pulled up next to Tommy's. She noticed right away that Tommy's color was better, and his breathing appeared normal. He was sleeping soundly.

Maleva had brought more elderberry and tiptoed out of the room. She found a hospital nun and gave her the herbs, requesting that more tea be made and brought to the boy's room. Tommy's doctor was standing nearby, and when the hospital nun looked at him questioningly, he nodded briefly. Looking at the gypsy, he said, "Good morning, Maleva. We meet again. It seems as though the good people of Tremorna have more faith in your ways than in mine."

Maleva, although grinning, said rather pompously, "Aye, Doc. I've told ye afore—the ol' ways is always the best."

As they walked to Tommy's room together, the doctor said, "I looked in on Tommy earlier. He seems to be holding his own. I would have changed the dressing, but I hadn't any seaweed." He winked at Maleva and then laughed aloud as she pulled a huge wad of it from her satchel. "You are an astonishing woman, Maleva," he chuckled, shaking his head as they walked into Tommy's room.

Tommy woke up momentarily as they were changing his dressings. He glanced over at Sister Therese, puzzled that she should be here. "Where am I?" he asked no one in particular. "Why am I 'ere?" He tried to sit up, but a pain sliced unmercifully through his side. He laid back down. He lost unconsciousness again, just as Kerena awoke.

Later that morning, Sister Agnessa and Sister Hildegard came to check on Tommy. They brought a change of clothes for Sister Therese, along with one of Cook's famous pasties. The Reverend Mother asked if she could speak with Sister Therese alone. Sister Hildegard left the room to check with the hospital nun about speaking with the doctor.

Tommy was sleeping peacefully. Sister Agnessa asked Kerena if she had had a chance to speak to Tommy about his parentage. Kerena shook her head no. "I've thought about this moment so many times Sister, and still, I don' know how to begin." She looked into the Reverend Mother's eyes and asked, "How do I tell Tommy that 'is real name is Matthew or that Jeremy Dugan is 'is father or that I am 'is mother? How do I tell 'im why I felt I had to protect 'im from 'is father?" Kerena looked down at her hands and whispered, "Will he ever forgive me? I love him so much. I just wanted to keep him safe. How will he ever understand?"

Sister Agnessa took Kerena's shaking hands in hers. "My dear, everything you did—every decision you made—was made out of love for your child. If he doesn't see that right now, he will someday."

Kerena glanced over at Tommy. His eyes were open. "M-mother?" he whispered hoarsely.

"Oh, Tommy! Ye're awake!"

The Reverend Mother silently left the room, leaving them alone for the first time in a very long time, as mother and son.

EPILOGUE

Before the next assizes, Jock died of blood poisoning from his infected leg wound. Roger Hawker delivered the news to Sal. She was inconsolable. Her heart could not hold any more grief. He didn't tell her that Jock would most likely have been hung outside the gates of Newgate Prison for his crimes, had he not died. Sal closed the Owler for good and eventually went to live with her sister in Cadgwith.

Jeremy was tried, sentenced to ten years hard labor, and transported by convict ship to the penal colony of Australia.

Father Cotter was sentenced to three years in prison for his involvement in smuggling activities and for the manslaughter of Harry "Whistler" Drake. The court stayed its decision. He remained in the care of the St. Lawrence Lunatic Asylum in Bodmin, where he died a few years later.

Tommy survived his wounds after a long period of convalescence in hospital and then at Tremorna Orphanage. Even though he was no longer an orphan, Tommy was allowed to live there. No charges were brought against Tommy because his involvement in the smuggling ring couldn't be proven. Roger Hawker told Tommy fiercely that he and his men would be watching him very carefully. Tommy told Roger that his days of misbehaving were over, and he kept his promise. When he was 18, he was offered an apprenticeship with a local shipbuilder. He became quite skilled in the trade and was well-respected among his peers. With his earnings, he was eventually able to purchase his own shipyard near Newquay. He asked Winnie to marry him, and she accepted. Two years later they were blessed with a son, Jonah. Tommy took his father's last name of Dugan but couldn't bring himself to use the name Matthew.

After confessing her sins in front of a panel of stern bishops in London, Sister Therese was pardoned. Sister Agnessa invited her to stay at Tremorna Orphanage, and she eagerly accepted. She had found serenity in this calling and spent another 23 years at the orphanage. Tommy's relationship with his mother, although strained at first, grew more loving as the years progressed. Kerena visited Tommy and his family in Newquay often and loved playing with her grandson. She died peacefully at the age of 56.

Jeremy Dugan did not come back to Cornwall. He wrote to his son when the spirit moved him. He never received a reply. For the last time, Tommy didn't looked back.

Old Mr. Terwilliger loved to recount (in gory detail) the shocking and tragic events of Tremorna's "Holly Bay Massacre" to anyone who would listen.